CAUGHT IN CROSSFIRE . . .

Temple, Gabriel, and Cole had almost reached the Apaches horses when one of the braves spotted them. Temple heard the startled yell that exploded from his lips, watched him bend swiftly and snatch up the rifle lying at his feet. Then Temple fired from the hip as the remainder of the renegade party, aroused by the brave's shout, leaped to their feet. At once, they began to trigger their rifles and loose arrows. But by then Gabriel and Cole had their guns out and were making use of them.

Three of the braves were down when Temple heard the chorus of wild yells coming from below him in the wash Through the dust haze he could see a dozen or more figures rushing toward him. Apaches! Now he and the others had only one choice—to forget the horses and run for their lives

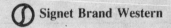 **Signet Brand Western**

Decision at Doubtful Canyon

by
Ray Hogan

Ⓢ

A SIGNET BOOK

NEW AMERICAN LIBRARY

TIMES MIRROR

PUBLISHED BY
THE NEW AMERICAN LIBRARY
OF CANADA LIMITED

NAL BOOKS ARE AVAILABLE AT QUANTITY DISCOUNTS WHEN USED
TO PROMOTE PRODUCTS OR SERVICES. FOR INFORMATION PLEASE
WRITE TO PREMIUM MARKETING DIVISION. THE NEW AMERICAN LI-
BRARY. INC.. 1633 BROADWAY. NEW YORK. NEW YORK 10019

First Printing, November, 1981

2 3 4 5 6 7 8 9

SIGNET TRADEMARK REG. U.S. PAT. OFF. AND FOREIGN COUNTRIES
REGISTERED TRADEMARK – MARCA REGISTRADA
HECHO EN WINNIPEG, CANADA

SIGNET, SIGNET CLASSICS, MENTOR, PLUME, MERIDIAN
and NAL BOOKS are published in Canada by The New American
Library of Canada, Limited, Scarborough, Ontario

PRINTED IN CANADA
COVER PRINTED IN U.S.A.

Publisher's Note

1

A bullet whipped at John Temple's shirt sleeve. Reacting, he crouched lower over his horse as it raced to reach the shelter of the brush and rocks a long fifty yards ahead. Twisting about, he looked back. The Apaches—a half dozen near-naked braves—had not gained on him in the last quarter mile. A hard grin split his mouth; if his luck held and he made it to the tangled brake, he'd have a good chance of shaking the renegades and getting them off his heels.

Another bullet slammed into the horn of his saddle and went screaming off into the early morning air. The braves had ceased their blood-curdling yells and were now concentrating on stopping him before he could gain the safety of the brake. Again Temple looked back. One of the Apaches had pulled slightly forward of his companions, had his rifle up, and was endeavoring to level the weapon for a third shot.

Temple drew his pistol, a well-used Colt cap-and-ball that had been altered by the Thuer Company to take forty-four caliber metallic cartridges. The range was a bit far for a hand gun, he knew, but getting to his rifle was not practical at the moment, and he just might distract the brave long enough to spoil his aim—probably none too good from the back of his onrushing pony anyway—and buy a little more of the time necessary to reach the deep brush.

Steadying the pistol as best he could, Temple threw a shot at the Indian. The Apache drew up suddenly, and for a long breath Temple thought he'd hit the renegade. But it wasn't so. The slug had apparently struck somewhere close, probably a stride or two ahead of the brave's straining pony, and the spurt of sand had caused the Apache to flinch.

Grim, Temple glanced once more at the brake to judge the distance that separated him from escape or capture. The ragged expanse of arroyos, bluffs, stunted trees, and dense undergrowth was no more than a dozen yards away. His hopes rose. He should be able to—

Temple felt the horse beneath him shudder and start to fall. Anger rocked through him. The damned Apache renegade had managed to put a bullet in the gelding! The desperate race insofar as the horse was concerned had ended. Abruptly the animal's head dipped forward and his legs buckled. Temple, dropping the reins, jumped clear of the falling horse.

He heard the Apaches' triumphant yells as he struck the ground feet first and went head over heels and down full length. Pain shot through his lank body like a stab of light, but he ignored it, his mind set wholly on escape—on survival.

On his feet instantly, he bent low and legged it for the nearest outcropping of brush. The brave with the rifle, evidently the only one armed with such, laid another shot at him. Temple heard the flat slap of the bullet as it smashed into a rock on his left and then its screech as it ricocheted off into space.

The brush closed in behind him, bringing a disappointed howl from the renegade Indians. But he was far from safe, Temple knew. Still hunched low and running hard, heedless of the noise he was making, he cut sharp right for a short distance, veered left into a narrow wash, and plunged on.

Well into the confusion of rocks, oak brush, plume, and other scrubby growth, Temple slowed, began to pick his way along more quietly. He could hear nothing of the Apaches, but by then they would be moving in and out of the brake searching for his trail. One of them would have paused at his dead horse to grab his rifle, the weapon being the principal cause for the attack, it and the fact that he was a white man in a part of the country the redmen—all treaties to the contrary—still felt was exclusively theirs.

Sucking deep for wind and swiping at the sweat beading over his eyes, Temple halted behind a mound of rocks and weeds to listen, hopeful of locating the Indians. At first he could hear nothing, only the drone of insects and the distant mourning of a dove, and then a yell echoed through the quiet. Such could only mean that one of the braves had picked up his trail and that the entire party would now be pressing forward. That was good; at least they would be bunched, and the possibility of eluding them would be much better than if they had scattered and were filtering singly through the brush and rocks.

Still breathing hard, Temple gave his position thought The braves would quickly find his tracks in the sandy arroyo into which he had turned and hurriedly cover its length. It would be wise to cut away now, keep on hard ground where signs of his passing would not be so easily found, and double back once he was certain he was well clear of their approach

It was like the war all over again, he thought, as he

cautiously but hurriedly moved on—like the time a Reb patrol had spotted him and several other Yankee soldiers in the thick woods near Spottsylvania Court House. He and the men with him, cut off from their Union regiment, had managed to avoid a division of Confederates by working their way in and out of the dense brush and trees. The attempt to escape entirely had failed when they walked into a trap laid by another party of Rebs, who, hearing their approach, had waited in ambush. The war had ended there for John Temple and the men with him for they had been quickly passed back through the lines to one of the Confederate prisons where they had remained until the conflict was over.

He'd not let himself be taken this time, however, Temple assured himself grimly. Being a prisoner of the Rebs was bad enough, but falling into the hands of Apache renegades was something no white man was likely to survive. He would do his best to shake them, but if he failed and was forced to make a stand—the only answer was a fight to the death.

Gliding silently along through the shadowy brush, avoiding loose rock that could dislodge and set up a noise that would give him away, Temple pressed on, moving in a wide circle. The Indians would be having trouble now picking up his trail in the dense growth. The ground underfoot was hard, littered with decaying leaves and other forest debris which would leave little if any evidence of his passing. It would be mostly sheer luck if they, skilled trackers that they were, located his trail.

He wished it were possible to return to his horse and recover his belongings. Everything he owned, except what he had on him, was on the gelding—extra clothing, slicker, spare cartridges for both his pistol and rifle, blanket roll, grub sack, and of course his saddle and like gear.

But to save his hide Temple reckoned he could get along without all of it, although he did regret losing the rifle. His money, about four hundred dollars, was safe inside the belt he was wearing, and the loops of his gun belt were all, but a half dozen or so, filled He was lucky to be alive, he supposed, but he was not out of danger yet.

The answer, of course, was to keep moving. He realized he was still a considerable distance from his goal, the Mexican border and he'd not likely make it there on foot before Ford Kailer and the Pinkerton Detective Agency man, Amos Bell caught up with him.

Temple gave that thought as he hurried on, angling now to his left—to the east. The two men who were trailing him had been fortunate, he guessed. They couldn't have been too far behind him when the Apaches had suddenly appeared, riding out of a grove of trees along which he was passing, and given chase

Each party had been unaware of the other, apparently, and the two men, seeing the braves, no doubt had quickly ducked back into some convenient shelter and wisely let the Indians take over. They would bide their time, wait to see if the Apaches succeeded in running him down, and if it developed that he had escaped, they would resume the chase that they had begun weeks ago—and sworn never to forsake until they had either captured or killed him.

There was one good thing to be said for the abrupt appearance of the Apaches. Kailer and Bell were being forced to back off and stand by until they knew how things turned out for him. Until they were certain one way or the other and believed also that it was safe to move on, they would lie low; and that would afford him time, since he was now on foot, to get them off his trail.

A hard grin once more crossed Temple's angular face. He was looking mighty far ahead for a man who still had a half-dozen redskins snapping at his heels! It just might work out that he'd never make it to where Bell and Kailer could resume dogging his tracks.

Temple came to a stop at the edge of a small clearing to once again recover his breath, try to determine where he was, and decide in which direction he should go. A few minutes earlier he had heard a shout from one of the Apaches. It had come from well beyond where he now was, and from that he reckoned the braves had overshot him; but there was no guarantee that such was true

A thin wisp of white smoke twisting up into the clear blue of the sky in the east caught Temple's attention. It seemed to originate at the extreme end of the brush and other growth which thrust forward to a point. There looked to be more trees in the spur, and from that he guessed it was a ranch house or perhaps a homesteader's place. Either one, it offered the possibility of obtaining another horse along with gear and grub that would be necessary if he were to make it to the Mexican border

Hope lifting within him, John Temple spent another two minutes listening for sounds of the Apaches and, hearing none, set out at a trot for the smoke streamer.

2

It was not a ranch or a homestead Temple saw as he drew near the collection of decaying structures. Judging from the size of the now empty corrals, the large barn which had lost its doors, the deserted smithy, and the extensive rambling main house, it once had been an important way station for stagecoaches—but no longer.

Disappointed, Temple moved slowly on to where he could see the front of the sagging building and there halted. The place was called Cottonwood according to the faded sign on its warped facade. He'd get no horse there, Temple realized, and unless the way station was still on a stagecoach route of some kind, he would be faced with a serious problem.

Throwing a glance over his shoulder and seeing no indication of Ford Kailer and Amos Bell—or of the Apaches—he crossed the sunbaked hardpack to the station. As he pulled back the screen door, the attached bell jangled noisily. Stepping inside, he halted. Two other persons—an attractive girl of eighteen or so and a man several years her senior, undoubtedly her brother from the resemblance—were sitting on a bench marked *Passengers*. A flow of relief swept through Temple; evidently the old way station was still a coach stop.

"Something for you, mister?"

The voice came from the opposite side of the room. Temple, taking note of the sparsely stocked shelves and concluding the place was also a general store of sorts, came around slowly.

"When's the next stagecoach due?"

A hunched shape materialized from the shadows beyond a counter along a wall and became an elderly man in baggy canvas pants supported by red suspenders, a colorless linsey-woolsey shirt, and run-down boots. Pointing a gnarled finger at the bench, he said, "One heading south for Doubtful Canyon'll be along directly. Set yourself down if you're of a mind to take it. Fare'll be two dollars."

Temple nodded, handed over the necessary fee, and, ignoring the passenger waiting-bench, moved over to a small, glassed-in case containing plugs of chewing tobacco, the makings for cigarettes, and a box of stogies.

"Can use a few of those," he said, pointing at the slim black cheroots.

The storekeeper's attitude of indifference altered perceptibly, and, hurrying in behind the counter upon which the case sat, he drew back its hinged top and exposed the stogies.

Temple gathered up a half dozen, thrust them into the pocket of his shirt, and laid a silver dollar on the counter.

"I don't suppose there's a chance of you having a horse around here somewhere you'd sell," he said hopefully.

The storekeeper made change for the dollar from a tin box and handed the coins to John Temple.

"Everything I got's for sale—but I sure ain't got no

horse," he said and then as a frown crinkled his narrow features and a puzzled look came into his eyes, added, "If you ain't got a horse, how'd you get here?"

"Walked," Temple said blandly, thrusting one of the cigars into his mouth. "Apaches shot mine out from under me."

The man on the bench came to attention. "Where?" he asked, rising.

"Brakes—west of here—"

"Big party of them?"

Temple, having licked the wrapper of the stogie, bit off its closed end and spat it aside. Striking a match he held it to the tip and sucked the weed into life. The man awaiting the stage, taking Temple's deliberateness as a refusal to answer his question, spoke up again.

"Ain't just being nosy, friend. My name's Morgan Cole, and this here's my sister, Laurie. Reason I'm wanting to know about the Apaches is we—our pa—has a ranch over thataway—on west of the brakes. We've been having plenty of trouble with them lately."

"There was only about a half a dozen in the bunch that jumped me," Temple replied. "Doubtful Canyon. That a town?"

"Kind of, but mostly it's a way station for the east- and west-bound stages, not just a stop like Farley's here."

"Them redskins get everything you had?" the store-keeper-agent, whose name evidently was Farley, wanted to know.

"All but what I'm wearing. . . . That stagecoach be in soon you think?"

Farley's stooped shoulders stirred. "Due right now, but it ain't always on time. Fact is, I ain't never for sure it's coming a'tall!"

Temple frowned, but before he could make further comment, Laurie Cole spoke up. Her voice was thick with sarcasm.

"Oh, it'll be along all right! Pa made sure of that before he sent Morgan and me over here to wait for it."

Morgan favored his sister with a dark look. "What she means is this is sort of an irregular run—only makes the trip from Pastor Valley to Doubtful Canyon when they've got passengers to haul. I'm taking my sister there and putting her on the eastbound coach for St. Louis. She's going to be attending school back there."

"Maybe," Laurie said coolly and turned her attention to the doorway and the long sloping hills beyond.

"Ain't no maybe about it!" Morgan Cole snapped. "You're going to do just what Pa tells you—and I aim to see that you do!"

"Maybe," the girl said again with infuriating calmness.

"Don't give me that!" Morgan countered harshly. "You're going to that school like Pa wants, and that's all there is to it! And if you're still thinking on running off with that Harley Edge—forget it! Pa give me orders to keep him away from you, and I sure figure to do it—even if I have to use a gun!"

"I guess you can try," Laurie said in the same serene, icy tone. "You'll do whatever Pa tells you to do—even jump off Piñon Ridge bluff if he says to—"

Morgan Cole's anger colored his face. He looked away. Temple, now beginning to feel a bit embarrassed at being witness to a family quarrel of no small consequence it would seem, turned away and sauntered toward a table in the rear of the room.

"Can pour you a cup of coffee," Farley said, following, and when Temple nodded, continued on through a curtained doorway into the area beyond—his living quarters, apparently.

Temple sat down and puffed on his cigar, realizing only then how good it was to get off his feet after the long, hurried flight through the brake to escape the Apaches. He hoped the stagecoach wouldn't be late. There were still Kailer and Amos Bell to bear in mind. If the Indians hadn't spotted them, they could be showing up before long, assuming they were aware of the direction he had taken. Of course, if they had run afoul of the Apaches, it could mean his problems with the two men were over and that there was no need for haste; but there was no way of knowing for certain at that moment just where he stood, and he could take nothing for granted.

Farley appeared, brushing aside the heavy green portiere with an elbow and carrying a mug of coffee in each hand.

"You be wanting sugar? Ain't got no milk since my old cow died—'cepting that canned stuff that ain't fit to use," he said as he placed one of the cups before Temple.

"Take mine black, no sugar," he said, glancing at the Coles, still quarreling but now in low undertones.

"Same here," Farley said and sat down. "If I ain't being nosy, where was you headed when them redskins jumped you?"

Temple gave that thought as he took a long sip of the chicory—strong, black, and evidently from a pot that had been simmering on the back of a stove for a considerable length of time.

"Arizona," he said, deciding it was better to avoid the truth. Kailer and Bell, if they had managed to stay

11

clear of the Apaches and came here looking for him, would be asking questions.

"Sure a lot of folks going over that way," the storekeeper said. "Must be a powerful lot of work to be had."

Temple shrugged. "Some, I expect, but the fact is there ain't much doing anywhere. War's been over three years, and things still ain't much going on."

Farley, toying with his cup, nodded. "It sure put a lot of folks out of business and set a'plenty of men looking for jobs, that's for dang sure. You a cowhand?"

Temple smiled bleakly. "Reckon I'm just about anything a job would call for. Grew up on a farm. Expect I know that best, but I've done my share of fence-riding and cleaning out water holes."

"Like as not Morgan's pa could use you," Farley said. "He's got the biggest ranch in these parts, and, being the devil hisself to work for, he's always needing hired hands."

Temple ducked his head slightly at Cole and his sister Laurie. "Sort of gathered that from listening to them," he said and then added, "Obliged to you for the suggestion, but I've sort of set my mind, so I reckon I'll keep on moving. Ain't never been no hand to switch once I'd decided on doing something."

"Know what you mean," Farley said, nodding. "And I sure do agree. If I hadn't gone and changed my mind once, I wouldn't be roosting here in this God-forsaken hole today!"

Temple removed the stogie from his mouth, exhaled a cloud of smoke, and taking up his cup downed its contents in a single gulp. Then, returning the empty mug to the table, he rose, strolled to a nearby window, and put his attention on the stretch of winding road to the north. The hope that the stagecoach would arrive soon was still high in his mind, pressing him with an urgency that tightened the lines of his features and brought a measure of concern to his gray eyes.

Tall, dark-haired, wind- and sun-tanned, his beard was a dark shadow on the lower half of his face, while a full brush mustache graced his upper lip. There was a tautness to him along with a kind of moody reserve as if he placed little faith or trust in anyone and cared little if anything about friendship.

Despite the growing heat he still wore the light wool poncho he'd pulled on early that morning as protection against the chill. Beneath it was a dark shirt, and the pants he wore were old army-issue as were his scarred boots and battered campaign hat. A red bandanna, the only item on him that looked to be fairly new, was about his neck.

There was a hard set to his jaw, and his lips maintained a straight, uncompromising line which furthered an impression of strength and self-assurance which, in turn, inspired confidence.

Suddenly he straightened. A boil of dust, well off in the distance but on the winding road to the north, caught his attention. It could be the coach—or it could be Kailer and Amos Bell, having cut away from the flats onto the better-traveled route. But it was not they he saw a few moments later with relief.

"Reckon this here's your stagecoach," he said, glancing at Farley.

The combination merchant and agent got to his feet and took up a stand beside Temple at the window.

"Yep, it sure is," he said and then, leaning forward, squinted at the oncoming vehicle.

"There's been trouble!" he added in a rising voice and wheeled for the door. "Looks like Abe Valentine, the driver, is all right, but Luke Walters, the shotgun, is laying all sprawled out, half off the seat!"

3

Both of the Coles—the girl most attractive in a gray traveling dress, piped jacket, scarf, and brown shoes— were on their feet and moving toward the entrance of the old way station with Farley. Temple, relieved when it became apparent that the dust cloud was not the two men trailing him but the stagecoach, now wondered if the trouble the coach had encountered was of such serious nature that the driver, Abe Valentine, Farley had called him, would refuse to continue on to the next stop.

"Looks like Walters is dead all right," he heard the agent say as the stage whirled in closer. "Got passengers inside too. Sure hope there ain't none of them hurt."

The coach, one of the lightweight rigs known as Celerity wagons, would offer little, if any, protection for those aboard in the event of attack. Built for use in sandy or mud-plagued country, it had no thick, molded-wood sides as did the Concords but instead used pull-down canvas curtains. Effective against the weather, the shades were useless when it came to stopping bullets or arrows.

The vehicle was being drawn by a team of four good horses, however, and it was likely that they, running fast and untiringly, were the reason the Celerity got through the attack at all.

"Indians!" Valentine yelled as he brought the coach to a sliding, almost sideways stop in front of the station. "Luke got hisself killed first off! Think one of my passengers is shot too!"

At that moment the curtains on the near side of the coach parted and were flung up. There were four passengers, all men, Temple saw, and one—a cattleman from the looks of him—was wounded. Blood crusted the right sleeve of his coat just below the shoulder.

He was followed by a well-dressed individual wearing a narrow-brimmed city hat and a blue, somewhat rumpled suit. He was unarmed whereas the rancher wore a belted gun.

The remaining two passengers emerged more slowly. The first to step down was a hard-faced man with sly black eyes, scruffy brown hair, a ragged beard and mustache. Handcuffs linked his wrists.

Close on his heels came an elderly lawman somewhere in his late sixties whose nickeled star read *Town Marshal* Temple studied him warily, but the marshal, who had a tough, no-nonsense way about him, appeared interested only in his prisoner.

He, too, had small dark eyes, but his hair was snow white, as were his mustache and beard. Clad in cord pants tucked into polished boots, a fringed leather jacket white shirt complemented by a black string tie, and a flat-crowned plainsman-style hat, he wore his holstered pistol on the outside. As he reached out, placed a veined hand on his prisoner's shoulder, and shoved him roughly toward a bench placed in front of the way station, Temple glimpsed the slight bulge of a belly gun tucked well back on his left side.

"Get yourself inside, mister," Temple heard Farley say to the wounded man. "There's medicine and such in the back room. I'll come do what I can for you soon as I help Abe get Luke down off'n the seat."

Laurie Cole moved quickly up to the door. She motioned to the cattleman. "I'll take care of you—"

"Name's Gabriel—Tom Gabriel," the man replied and, holding his injured arm, followed the girl into the store.

"Where'd them devils jump you?" Farley asked as he and Valentine, a squat, bowlegged oldster in leather breeches and vest, began to work at removing the body of the unfortunate shotgun that had become wedged between the dashboard and the seat of the coach.

"Was right after I got into Sunflower Canyon, where all them trees are up close to the road. About a dozen in the bunch. The bastards come a'sailing out from both sides at us. Luke got hit right then. Hadn't been for Marshal Kelley and that rancher, Gabriel, I misdoubt we'd ever made it here. . . . You mind giving us a hand here, mister?" Valentine added, glancing over his shoulder at John Temple. "Seems Luke weighs about a ton!"

Temple stepped up quickly and, climbing onto the seat of the Celerity, added his efforts to those of Farley and Abe Valentine in lifting the dead guard from his locked-in position and then off the coach.

"Where we putting him?" the driver asked as he and the storekeeper lugged the limp body of Walters toward the station.

"Round back—that'll be best. You figure I ought to bury him here, or has he got folks back at Pastor Valley who'll want to see to that?"

"Luke didn't have nobody, far as I know," Abe said

as they rounded the corner of the building and headed for its rear.

The city man had trailed Laurie Cole and the rancher Gabriel into the station and was waiting somewhere inside. Morgan Cole, too, had reentered the building. Not too anxious to give the lawman Kelley a good look at himself, Temple followed, entering just as the storekeeper-agent and the stagecoach driver, relieved of their burden, came in the back way.

"How long we going to hang around here?"

It was Kelley's voice, coming from the front doorway. "Important I get Philbin to the sheriff at Grant soon as possible."

Valentine, wiping at his face and neck with a bandanna, shook his head.

"Now, you just hold your horses, Marshal! I'll get you there fast as I can." The old driver paused and glanced at the Coles. Laurie had finished bandaging Tom Gabriel's arm, helped him with his coat, and now was standing near her brother in the center of the room.

"You folks passengers?"

Morgan nodded. Farley jerked a thumb at Temple. "Him too. Makes three wanting to go to Doubtful Canyon."

Valentine tucked his bandanna into a back pocket. "Tots up to seven—"

"Can count me out," the man in city clothing broke in. "I think I'll hang around here for a spell—a day or two—sort of let things settle down."

"Now, just what things you talking about?" Valentine demanded.

"My nerves, mostly—I just ain't used to being shot at. Maybe by the time the next stagecoach comes along the Indians will all have gone."

"Ain't likely," the driver said with a shrug, "but you suit yourself. I'll be coming back through in a couple of days and can haul you back to Pastor Valley—but them redskins'll still be hanging around."

"What're the chances of us running into them on the way to Doubtful Canyon?"

"Better'n good," Valentine said flatly. "Hell, you can just about figure on running into a bunch of them anywhere in this country right now."

"I heard the tribes were all peaceable—"

"Reckon they are, but young bucks don't pay no mind to the old chiefs. There's maybe a dozen bunches of them—renegades they are—out roaming around looking to jump pilgrims and stagecoaches like us. They're even raiding small ranches and homesteaders."

"Been expecting them to pay me a visit," Farley said wryly. "Ain't safe around here nowhere right now."

The city man turned away. "Guess I'll lay over like I mentioned," he said and faced Farley. "You be able to put me up?"

The storekeeper nodded. "I've got a room out back with a cot in it. Can use that."

"How about the rest of you folks?" Abe Valentine asked and settled his attention on Morgan Cole. "You aiming to chance your wife by going—"

"Happens she's my sister—not my wife," Cole answered stiffly. "And we'll be going on. Important we make it to Doubtful Canyon, too."

"Up to you—but I'll be needing somebody to ride shotgun for me."

There was a silence broken finally by Gabriel who said, "Don't think I'd be much good to you, driver—"

"Nope, reckon you wouldn't with that arm all bunged up," Valentine said and glanced around. "Well, somebody sure better speak up! I ain't pulling out without somebody a'setting up there on the box with me. Now, the marshal's got his hands full with his prisoner, and that there other fellow's got to look out for his sister. That leaves you, friend," the old driver concluded, looking at Temple.

"All right with me," John Temple replied, tossing aside his half-finished cigar. He was willing to comply with any request that would get him on the way before Amos Bell and Ford Kailer put in an appearance.

Valentine considered Temple appraisingly and tugged at an end of his stringy mustache. "Expect you'll do fine," he said and began to draw on his leather gloves. "You aiming to tie your horse on behind?"

"He ain't got one," Farley volunteered. "That's what he's going to Doubtful Canyon for—to get hisself something to ride."

Valentine again studied Temple, this time a bit more closely. Undoubtedly he was wondering why he, clearly a man on the move, was on foot in a land where a horse was an absolute necessity.

"Apaches got his'n—shot it right out from under him," Farley explained. "Come here looking to buy one. Told him his best bet was Doubtful Canyon."

Valentine shrugged. "Yeh, it will be," he said and then added, "When we get there, mister, talk to Dave Christman—he's the agent. Tell him you're wanting to buy a horse."

"He still got some of them pony express animals around?" Farley asked.

"Reckon he has—about a half a dozen. Good horse-flesh too, even if they are maybe ten years old or so. If you want—say, what is your name?"

"Temple—"

20

"If you want, Temple, I'll talk to Dave. Tell him to make you a good deal seeing as how you're a'doing us a big favor to ride shotgun."

"I'll be obliged," Temple said, waiting for the driver and the passengers to move toward the door.

Valentine slapped his gloved hands together. "Well, climb aboard, folks," he said. "We're running a mite late, and I aim to make up a bit of time."

4

As he drew himself up onto the seat of the coach beside Abe Valentine, who was gathering up the lines of the four-horse hitch and kicking off the brake with a booted foot in preparation to move out, John Temple swept the country to the west and north for a sign of riders. There were none to be seen, and, satisfied, he settled down next to the old driver.

At that moment Valentine shouted a command to his team, and the coach lunged into forward motion as the horses responded.

"Where's the rifle?" Temple asked, glancing about.

Valentine—the team now stretched out and running hard—turned his attention to the boards beneath his feet. He swore loudly and shook his head.

"Luke must've dropped the dang thing when he got shot!" he replied, yelling to make himself heard above the thunder of the horses' hooves, the grating of the coach's iron-tired wheels in the sandy soil, and the constant creaking and popping. "Reckon you'll just have to use that six-shooter of your'n if we get jumped again."

Temple made no reply. Holding off an attack on the coach with a pistol would work as long as the Indians were near. It would take a rifle to make them keep their distance, however.

Bending over, Temple had a look at the side of the coach. The passengers had dropped the curtain lifted back at Cottonwood to shut out as much as possible of the thin yellow dust boiling around the vehicle. With all the curtains down and fastened securely at the bottom, the coach would be fairly tight.

'You ever ride shotgun before?''

Abe Valentine, sitting slightly forward on the box, arms sawing rhythmically from the bobbing pressure of the horses' heads as they put their backs to climbing a small hill, voiced his question in a shout.

'Once or twice,'' Temple responded, also raising his tone.

''Around these parts?''

''No, up Dakota way.''

''Figured that. I know just about every jasper who ever had anything to do with stagecoaching, from the jehus on down to the stable hands, around here. Drove for Butterfield for a spell, then with Wells Fargo. After I quit them I tied up with a couple of little jerkwater outfits like this'n . . . How long you been around here?''

''Just passing through—''

'Heading for California, I bet. Lon said the redskins got your horse—''

''Shot him out from under me early this morning.''

Valentine clucked sympathetically. ''Them devils, damn them to blazes! They're sure giving folks this side of the Mogollons a peck of trouble! Folks on the other side of the mountains ain't been bothered at all. . . . How many of them was there in the bunch that tied into you?''

23

"Half a dozen—"

"Hunting party," Valentine declared and fell silent while he shook out his lines. The team had topped out the grade and was beginning the roll down the opposite side. "Was a dozen or more took out after us."

Again the talkative old driver lapsed into silence while he tended his onrushing team. Then, 'Sure do hate that about Luke. Expect he never knew what hit him. One minute he was setting there right where you are, and the next one, he was pure dead. Sure is the way for a man to go, howsomever, if he's bound to cash in. Quick and easy. No dragging on sick and putting folks to a lot of trouble—ain't that right?"

"It is for certain," Temple replied.

"You know any of them folks we got inside?"

Temple shook his head. They were rolling down the grade at a fast clip, and he wondered if Abe Valentine, perhaps, wasn't being a bit conservative with the brake. A coach could gain so much momentum at such times that it would begin to overtake the horses, start to sway and could overturn. He'd seen it happen before, but he reckoned Abe Valentine, who undoubtedly had made the Cottonwood—Doubtful Canyon run many times, knew what he was doing.

"No. All strangers to me."

"Same here," Valentine said. "Have heard about them Coles—Lon Farley mentioned them to me. Their pa's got a big spread over in the Chamisa Hills country The gal's sure a mighty pretty little thing. Don't think that boy's much. Hear his pa keeps him cut down to buttonsize all the time. Won't let him do nothing but what he tells him to do."

"You know that marshal?" Temple asked.

"Ira Kelley? No, not real good. Comes from some

24

place north of Pastor Valley—that's where I'm living. It's where this here stagecoach comes from too, in fact. That sonofabitch he's taking to the sheriff at Grant—he's a real bad one, they say. Killed himself three or four men and some women.''

"Women?"

''Yep. He's one of them kind that likes to find some homesteader's or maybe a rancher's wife at home alone. It's a shame some husband didn't catch up with the bastard and kill him before the law nailed him. Would've saved a hanging. You know, there ain't nothing worse'n one of his kind that takes advantage of a woman.''

'For sure,'' Temple agreed. His voice had lowered and a bleakness had come into his eyes, filling them with a hard, unforgiving quality.

''Reckon Kelley'll be mighty glad to hand Philbin over to that sheriff. He's plenty skittish about the whole thing. Thinks Clint's friends are aiming to bust him loose somewheres along the line before we get to Doubtful Canyon—and Grant.''

''Been wondering—why is the place called Doubtful Canyon?''

They had came off a rolling prairie and were now beginning to descend into a vast, ragged area of red bluffs and buttes where brush grew thick and the only trees in evidence were deep green, squat junipers.

Valentine, again letting the team have their way, cocked one foot on the brake and, leaning forward, wiped his mouth with the back of a hand.

''It's a pass in the old Peloncillos—the mountains west of it. Folks got to calling it that because getting through it was always mighty doubtful on account of the Apaches.''

''You ever have trouble there?''

25

"Nope—never was on that run. It's the line going west into the new territory—Arizona, but I know a few jehus that did. Any man handling the lines on that route was powerful glad once he was through the pass."

"How about this run? You ever get hit by Indians along here?"

"Couple, maybe three, times as I recollect. Big reason I wasn't in no hurry to leave Cottonwood without a shotgun setting up here on the box with me. Was lucky them other times, but that can change—luck, I mean—and I ain't never been no hand to sort of help it along."

"Looks like good country for an ambush," Temple said, letting his glance drift over the rough, broken area.

"For damn sure—here and a bit farther on. Last time they come at me was on the yonder side of Coyote Wash. Just happened I had me four soldier boys riding in the coach, and them and Luke sure made them stinking redskins change their minds in a hurry! Was better'n a dozen of them in the bunch, and before they got it figured out that they'd come up against a buzz saw, half of them was cold dead."

"How long ago was that?"

"About six months. Things sort of quieted down after that. The army met with the chiefs of most of the tribes, and they patched up their differences. But trouble is there's always a few bucks—and it ain't always the young ones—that won't go along with their chief and take off on their own."

Abe Valentine paused, raised himself slightly off the seat, and looked beyond the bobbing heads of the lead horses. A few moments later he settled back, satisfied evidently with what he did or did not see.

"Them's the devils that gives us trouble," he resumed.

"Always sneaking up on some rancher or homesteader and raiding and then burning the place or maybe jumping on some pilgrims or stopping a stagecoach. The chiefs don't know nothing about their doings—leastwise they claim they don't."

"Can find renegades among the whites, too."

"Ain't denying that! Got that Clint Philbin that Kelley's taking to Grant for proof of that!"

"Heard you mention Grant before. It a town somewhere near Doubtful Canyon?"

"A ways east of it," Valentine said and once again brushed at the dust on his mouth. The road was gunpowder dry, and the haze churned up by the horses and the wheels of the Celerity swirled about the coach in a reddish cloud.

Temple was beginning to feel the choking effect too and working some slack into his neckerchief pulled it up over his nose and mouth.

"Hear some fellows are aiming to do some mining for silver around there—around Grant. Ain't sure who or exactly where, but I've been told there's a whole passel of folks figuring to move into the country and start working . . . Ho, Jasper! Ho, Blackie! Easy—easy!"

The coach had begun to sway more than usual as it thundered onto an extra rough stretch of road. Someone inside the curtained vehicle yelled in protest as it rocked violently and slid sideways for a short distance amid a loud creaking and popping as if it were about to break apart. Righting itself, it rushed on, mounted a hump, and then dropped off into the trench beyond with a jarring thud that brought another shout from one of the passengers.

"Damn it!" Valentine swore. "That there washed-out place gets worse all the time! One of these here days I'm going to tote along a shovel and do some road fixing."

"A rough spot for sure," Temple agreed resettling himself.

Valentine tilted his weathered face and pointed ahead with his bewhiskered chin.

"That there's Porcupine Flats you're looking at. Once we climb out of this here canyon onto it, the going's real good."

"How far are we from Doubtful Canyon?"

"Well, I reckon we're about half way. We used to stop, breathe the horses about here, and let the passengers eat a lunch that Lon Farley put up for them. Things were good in those days. Lots of traveling down this way from the north—but then another stagecoach outfit come in and started using a different route, and business just dropped off so bad that the owners shut down the run."

"You driving for them then?"

"Nope, was working for Butterfield. Got kind of tired of driving and quit them and went back to my place in Pastor Valley. Folks got to bellyaching about not having no way to get to Doubtful Canyon so's they could make a connection with coaches going east or west or maybe on south.

"Fellow by the name of Holliday—owns the general store and one of the saloons in Pastor—decided maybe he could make some money running a stage back and forth, so he went out and bought this here Celerity and then talked me into driving it for him.

"Business weren't too bad at first—we was only making a run once a week—but then somebody, somewhere made a change again, and things went to hell, just like before. Only make the trip now when we've got passengers to haul, and that ain't even once a week sometimes.''

"How do you know when there's going to be somebody waiting at Cottonwood—like the Coles and me.''

"Don't, unless we get word. Folks around here have to sort of plan ahead and send us word—Cole had one of his cowhands ride by and leave word—that they want to get picked up. And now and then some drummer or maybe somebody like Marshal Kelley shows up wanting to get hauled to the junction. About you—you was just plain lucky to be there at the time I was making a run . . . Best you keep your eyes peeled from here on till we get up on the Flat. It'll be along here them danged redskins'll jump us if there's any around aiming to.''

"Good spot for it,'' Temple said, sweeping the country around them with eyes narrowed to cut down the dust.

The road at that point ran along the face of a steep slope which extended on above them to a high summit. On their left the grade dropped sharply away into a narrow canyon crowded with brush, rocks, and small juniper and piñon trees Little wonder it was a favorite place for marauding Indians to—

"Damn it—there they are!'' Abe Valentine yelled suddenly. "They're coming down on us from off the top of the hill!''

5

Temple swung his attention to the right. A dozen or so braves were surging out of the trees toward the road bent on heading off the coach. Drawing his pistol, Temple leaned down and slapped at the drawn curtain of the Celerity.

"Indians!" he shouted above the hammering hooves of the horses and the creaking of the coach. "Coming at us from the right—from the slope!"

Valentine was forward on the seat, lines laced through the fingers of his left hand, whip in the other.

"Go, Blackie! Jim!" he shouted as he plied the braided leather. "Run, you beauties! Ho, Jasper! Blue Boy! Go—damn you—go!"

Temple, half-erect, bracing himself by clinging to the baggage rail that had been added to the Celerity's top, steadied the pistol he was holding and waited for the braves to draw closer.

They were strung out in a line, he saw, and were sweeping down on the coach at a fast run. Sun glinted off their copper, half-naked bodies, and the hills were echoing with their shrill yells. Some carried rifles—about half of them he thought; the remainder were armed with bows and arrows.

"Eleven," he muttered, counting for no good reason. "Eleven of them—"

The sharp crack of a gunshot coming from inside the coach broke Temple's concentration. Leaning down again he shouted, "Hold your fire! Let them get closer!"

The shot was hardly noticed by the renegade braves Bent low over their ponies' necks, heels drumming the ribs of the animals, they came on.

"They're aiming to get us at the curve!" Abe Valentine shouted. "Got to beat them damn redskins to it!"

The curve   Temple threw his glance beyond the straining team The bend in the road made a sharp cut to the right not far ahead. At that particular point the coach would need to slow drastically; otherwise, momentum would swing it wide, and the probability of going over the edge down onto the floor of the canyon some fifty feet or more below was almost a certainty.

"We'll never make it!" Temple shouted back. "We're going too fast!"

Valentine did not take his narrowed eyes off the road and, still half-erect, using the whip mercilessly shook his head.

"You best leave the driving to me! Your job's to do the shooting!"

The Apaches opened fire at that moment Bullets whined by overhead; one thudded into the wood of the dashboard, another ricocheted off a wheel's steel tire Temple took aim at a brave and pressed off a shot The lead slug was low and hit the Indian in the leg, wounding but not killing him. Immediately he swung away.

At Temple's shot the men inside the stage began to use their weapons—all pistols. Temple swore at the ill luck that denied him and the others a rifle But there

31

was no sense bemoaning the lack—they would simply have to do the best they could with handguns.

Another brave took a bullet. Throwing up his arms, ne rocked back on his horse, swayed briefly, and fell to the ground.

"Good! Good!" Abe Valentine cried as the coach, whipping from side to side, raced on. "You keep on doing that, partner, and we'll make it by them stinking devils!"

Temple was not sure it was he who had brought down the brave, as the men inside the stage were laying down a steady barrage—if the steady firing of three pistols could be termed such. But it didn't matter; what did was that the charging braves appeared to be slowing, to be breaking off.

It could be only to gain a better position, Temple realized moments later. The curve was now just ahead, no more than a hundred feet. Valentine had not let up on the horses, and now, on the slight incline leading into the bend, the Celerity began to rock and tip dangerously.

The Indians were in near enough to make use of their bows. Arrows now began to soar through the midday, dust-filled air. One struck the hindquarters of the off wheel horse and remained there, feathers fluttering, standing stiffly upright. Another buried itself in the baggage atop the coach, while a third pierced the thick curtain closing off the wagon's side.

Valentine recoiled. A red stain blossomed high on his chest where an Apache bullet had found its mark. The old driver cursed vividly and, leaning forward again, saw to his lines.

Suddenly the head of the near leader went down as a bullet drove into him. His legs seemed to freeze momentarily in midstride, and then abruptly the horse collapsed in a wild churning of dust. The coach slammed drunkenly from side to side, crowding the confused, frightened team, and shortly went over the edge of the road. It hung there, poised on the lip of the shoulder for a long breath, and then started down the slope in a bouncing, plunging descent.

Temple could hear Valentine cursing steadily, as futilely he continued to saw on the reins in a hopeless attempt to guide the frantic animals. Yells and screams were coming from inside the stage, and baggage loosened from the overhead rack was soaring off in all directions.

"Jump!" Temple shouted to Valentine as the unchecked plunging vehicle neared the bottom of the slope and reeled toward a tree.

He did not wait to see if the old jehu followed his advice but launched himself from the seat at a thick stand of rabbit brush. He struck hard, but the tough, stringy bushes broke the force of his fall and catapulted him clear onto the sandy bed of the wash running along the floor of the canyon.

Dazed, nevertheless, he pulled himself to his feet and stood for a long moment staring at the still spinning wheels of the overturned Celerity. Then as the curtains were flung back and the cattleman Tom Gabriel began to crawl into the open, Temple hurried forward to assist the man and those of the others who were still alive

Abe Valentine was dead, his neck broken in the fall, but it was likely the bullet he had taken would have brought death anyway. Laurie Cole was unhurt, thanks to the quick thinking of her brother Morgan, who, at the moment the coach started over the rim of the canyon on its erratic, downward course, had wrapped his arms about her and prevented her being thrown about inside the vehicle

Clint Philbin was knocked senseless but had quickly recovered his wits, hopeful no doubt that Marshal Ira Kelley was mortally injured. But the old lawman, while suffering a broken shoulder, was in no way about to give up his prisoner. Gabriel had sustained no further problems other than a bad shaking-up.

"I reckon we can thank them curtains for keeping us alive," he said, brushing absently at the dust on his coat. 'Wasn't for them we'd have all got thrown out and for certain killed."

Temple was only half hearing the man's comments. His eyes were on the road above, looking for the Indians he knew would be coming. At first he could not locate them, and then he saw the party riding hurriedly along the edge of the canyon looking for a less precipitous place where they could descend into the canyon and double back to their prize.

"Got to get out of here—quick," Temple said in a taut voice, moving to where Abe Valentine lay. "Those renegades'll be here in a few minutes."

Hoisting the old driver's slight figure onto his shoulders, he motioned to Cole and Gabriel. "Grab yourselves a couple of those branches that got busted off the bushes and wipe out our tracks."

Gabriel, reacting at once, seized a thick, leafy bit of the shrub, tossed it to Morgan Cole, and then took up another for himself. Nearby Ira Kelley, standing with his broken shoulder thrown forward at an odd angle as he pressed the muzzle of his pistol into the back of Philbin with his good hand, frowned through the pain that was showing on his lined face

34

"What're you aiming to do? Seems to me we'd best fort up right here—inside the coach."

"We wouldn't last ten minutes," Temple said in a quick, decisive sort of way as he started back up the canyon. "Smartest thing we can do is get as far away from here as we can, find a good place to hide—and hope those renegades are more interested in the wreck and the two horses that are still alive than they are in hunting us down "

6

They hurried off into the brush and rock, cautioned by John Temple to leave as little sign of their passage as possible. Both Morgan Cole and the cattleman Tom Gabriel took pains to brush out any footprints in the loose sand and occasional patches of soft soil. Fortunately the ground was well littered with leaves and other trash, and the job of covering up their trail was not too difficult.

"How far we going?" Clint Philbin demanded peevishly. "Them Indians ain't—"

"Until we find a safe place to hide," Temple cut in.

He paused to cast a glance at the now distant wrecked coach. The two horses that had survived the accident, still trapped in their harness, were standing patiently by the smashed Celerity awaiting attention. There was no sign yet of the Apaches; evidently they had had to travel a considerable way down the road to locate a point where they could manage the steep incline.

"Ain't going to make no difference what we do anyway," the outlaw grumbled. "Them redskins'll find us, sure as shooting. What we ought to do is climb up into them rocks over there and make a stand. If one of you's got an extra gun I'll—"

"If somebody has, you ain't going to get your hands on it!" Ira Kelley snapped.

Philbin swore. "Damn it all, a man's got the right to defend himself—specially against savages."

"I reckon he does," the lawman drawled, "but you ain't a man."

That he was suffering deeply from his broken shoulder was apparent to everyone, but the old marshal was not relenting in the least in his attitude toward his prisoner.

Cole and Gabriel, having finished with their chore to that point, drew up alongside Temple, sweating heavily from the weight of Valentine's body.

"You seen anything of them Indians yet?" the cattleman asked. He too was soaked with perspiration and breathing hard from his efforts.

Temple shook his head and shifted his burden to a more comfortable position. "No, but we can look for them to show up any minute."

"You figure there's any reason to go any farther?" the rancher continued. "We've put a fair piece of ground between us and them now."

"Rocks are bigger, and there's more of them on ahead," Temple replied, moving on. "We'll be better off if we go on to them."

A few minutes later Laurie Cole spoke up. "It looks like a cave up there," she said, pointing at a large slide of boulders to their right.

Without hesitation Temple veered toward the pile. No cave, it was a head-high triangular space between two massive rocks that showed signs of having been used as a shelter by both humans and wildlife at times during the past.

"Just what we're looking for," Temple said as he reached it.

Halting in the center, he leaned forward and allowed the lifeless body of Abe Valentine to slip from his shoulder to the ground. As the driver's leg lifted slightly during the process, a pistol dropped from its hiding place inside a boot.

Instantly Clint Philbin lunged for the weapon, but Ira Kelley threw himself at the outlaw and knocked him aside with his shoulder. The older man's face blanched with pain, but no sound escaped his tight lips, and as Temple reached down and recovered the weapon—an early model Starr forty-one caliber cap-and-ball—the lawman nodded coldly at Philbin.

"You try a stunt like that again, and I'll cave in your skull!"

The outlaw grinned. "You ain't going to do nothing, old man. Fact is, you're plain wasting your time. If you think you're going to get me to that tin badge in Grant, you best think again."

"I'll get you there," Kelley said softly. "One way or another, I'll get you there."

Temple, thrusting the old driver's pistol under his belt, moved over to where he could see the coach, barely visible now through the intervening brush. The Apaches had arrived and were closing in cautiously, evidently fearful of an ambush. They would be surprised and infuriated at finding no one—dead or alive.

Turning to the girl standing close by, Temple nodded to her. Her face was smudged from dust, and a sleeve seam in her jacket had parted. Otherwise she appeared no worse for the accident.

"Be obliged if you'll keep an eye on the Indians—let me know if any start this way—"

Laurie, her eyes a light blue in the strong sunlight,

smiled faintly and crossed to where she could do his bidding. Temple then wheeled quickly to the men

"Be a good idea to drag up some brush and stack it in front of the rocks—the cave," he said. 'If those Apaches don't find our tracks, there's better than a good chance they'll start hunting through the canyon for us. Could walk right past if we pile enough stuff up there "

"They won't find no tracks," Morgan Cole said firmly, moving off toward a pile of brush at the mouth of a nearby wash 'Me and Gabriel will guarantee that."

When the job of effectively covering the mouth of the cavelike opening between the rocks was completed through the efforts of Cole, the cattleman, and himself, Temple turned then to the job of disposing of Abe Valentine's body. He had been unwilling to leave it at the wreck site, fearing that the renegades would make sport of it.

"Look around for a place to bury the driver," he directed.

Cole complied at once, but Gabriel had turned to Ira Kelley and was doing what he could to ease the lawman's pain. Taking no chances while the rancher worked at setting the bone and improvising a sling, Kelley was holding his pistol on Clint Philbin— -eyes never wavering from the outlaw.

"Sort of a hole over there where I got some of that brush," Morgan Cole said, beckoning to Temple "Expect we could kind of clean it out and make it deep enough."

Temple paused to look at Laurie, still at her post. She shook her head when he caught her attention, and he moved on with Morgan, following the younger man to the specified place If some of the rocks and windblown rash were removed, it would do, he saw. He set to work immediately with the assistance of Cole, hollowed out a shallow grave, placed Abe Valentine's body in it, and covered it over with bits of leaves and brush, loose dirt, and stones—being careful to not click them together and thus set up a noise the Indians might hear.

It was a makeshift tomb for the old driver, but it was necessary something be done with Valentine's body in the steadily rising heat since there was no possibility of getting it back to his home in Pastor Valley. Securely under ground it would be safe from the coyotes and buzzards.

Yells were coming from the wrecked Celerity when he and Cole returned to the cave, and, crossing to Laurie at once, Temple took up a position beside her.

"They're still there," she said. "Just poking around in the wreck"

"Good," he murmured and looked her over more closely.

Even with the torn dress, the dust smudges, and disorderly hair, Laurie Cole was a very attractive woman, he saw. But there was more than just surface beauty, Temple suspected. He could see a firmness to her, a will that was not to be easily turned aside, and the steadiness of her gaze carried a warning that she was not to be underestimated in any way.

"Glad you didn't get hurt," he said then, his attention again on the Apaches.

She shrugged, her shoulders stirring slightly under the fabric of her gray dress and stylish jacket.

"I can thank my brother for that—but I expect it was more in the interest of getting me packed off to school than it was keeping me from being injured."

The bitterness in her voice brought a quick recollection

of the words that had passed between them back at Cottonwood. Temple shifted his attention to Morgan. He was leaning against one of the large rocks, wide-brimmed, high-crowned white hat pushed to the back of his head, his range clothing dusty but no worse than that from the accident. As Temple watched, Cole drew his pistol and checked its cylinder, making certain that it was fully loaded.

"Damn!" Temple heard Laurie say in a tight sort of voice. "Those Indians—they've got into my trunk and are going through my clothes, taking some of the dresses What would they want with them?"

"For their women—and they'll be using some of the colored stuff themselves," Gabriel, overhearing, ex-plained. "Some of it they'll use for bands around their heads, and if they come across a real bright piece that strikes their fancy, they'll use it to wrap around their middles—like a sash."

"Doesn't seem to bother them that they didn't find any of us there," Cole said, joining the group. 'You reckon they ain't going to bother tracking us down?"

"Not likely," Temple replied. "They'll rustle through all that baggage first—the spoils I guess you could call it—then they'll scatter and start looking for the passengers they knew were aboard the coach. They're in no hurry. Figure we've got nowhere to go, so they'll pick all the choice items that were in your baggage then go to hunting us."

There was a long silence broken finally by Ira Kelley "How many guns've we got?"

Temple didn't trouble to glance about to make a count. Gabriel and Morgan Cole were both wearing pistols, as were he and the lawman.

"Five, counting the one Abe was carrying—"

The lawman's face was grim. "Well, maybe we can give a pretty good account of ourselves if them savages find us." He paused, turned his small black eyes to Laurie. "Lady, can you shoot—shoot a pistol, I mean?"

"I know how," the girl replied. "Better with a rifle, but I expect I—"

"You just maybe will have to use that iron Temple's got there in his belt."

The yelling down at the scene of the wreck was continuing, now interspersed with much laughing. Glancing at the activity, Temple saw that one of the braves had taken a yellow petticoat of Laurie's, had draped it about his body, and was making a great show of whirling around to the amusement of his friends. But the braves were about finished with their prowling through the scattered belongings of the stagecoach passengers and were now beginning to drift about studying the ground for tracks that would tell them where their prospective prisoners had gone.

"Got them stumped," Gabriel said after a few moments had passed

"Won't be for long I expect," Temple said. "Can look for them to split up and strike out in all directions."

He was right. For a time the braves continued to search the immediate area of the wreckage, and then they all drew together for a discussion that lasted several minutes. When it ended, the party broke into pairs that began to work slowly through the brush on the floor of the canyon in a steadily widening circle as they sought to pick up some sign of the missing passengers.

"Best we get back in the cave," Temple said, his attention on two braves moving in their direction. "If they get suspicious and come in close, Cole and I will have to jump them. Don't want any shooting done, so

42

we'll use clubs. A gunshot will bring the others up fast.''

''If that happens we're sure in for one hell of a scrap,'' Marshal Kelley observed unnecessarily.

Temple nodded grimly as they returned to the space between the rocks. ''Stay down low,'' he warned as he selected two fairly thick tree limbs from the brush pile to serve as clubs and handed one to Morgan Cole. He would much prefer to have Tom Gabriel with him should the Apaches become suspicious and decide to investigate the rocks, but the rancher's wounded arm would hamper him in a hand-to-hand fight and everything would depend on their silencing the renegades quickly.

''They've spotted the brush—''

At Cole's tense words Temple shook his head. ''Don't talk. Maybe they'll pass us by.''

The two braves drew nearer, eyes on the ground probing the tangled growth to the sides and ahead of them. Once the shorter of the two halted, dropped to his haunches, and began to finger about in the litter as if he had found something of note. Apparently it was nothing of value, as he grunted something to his companion, rose, and resumed the search.

They drew abreast of the cave between the boulders but pressed on, seemingly intent on the heavy brush a dozen yards farther on. A shout from back somewhere near the wreck brought them to a stop. They remained motionless for a time, listening, and then, abruptly turning, started to retrace their steps at a trot.

''Now what the hell you reckon that's all about?''

At Ira Kelley's question Temple only shrugged. Morgan Cole said, ''One of them's found something—that's for sure.''

Temple moved to the outer edge of the brush where

he had a limited view of the braves, again gathered near the overturned Celerity. The two surviving horses had been cut free of their harness, he saw, and were being readied for leading off.

"Ain't doing nothing," Gabriel said, stepping in beside Temple. "Just standing there jabbering."

"Well, something's got into them," Morgan Cole said, adding his presence. "Either they've seen something, like maybe another party of Indians that they ain't friendly with, or could be the army."

"Either one suits me fine," Temple murmured.

"Looks like they're mounting up," Gabriel said.

Temple nodded in satisfaction. "Just set tight. Soon as they move out, I'll climb up on top of those big rocks where I can see good and make sure they keep going. Could be a trick to bring us out of hiding."

But the braves, for some unexplainable reason, rode on, Temple saw a quarter hour later when he had made it to the summit of the rocks he had indicated and could see the party of Apaches well in the distance. With the two stagecoach horses in tow, they were heading south. Returning to the cave, he reported to the others in his party.

"They're gone, that's for sure," he said. "Don't know yet why. Couldn't spot anybody else around."

"Who the devil can figure out what makes a redskin tick?" Marshal Kelley said in disgust. "Probably decided we wasn't worth the trouble of hunting down. Had all our belongings, anyway—"

"Except our guns," Temple added, "and that's what they wanted most. I think we ought to get back to the coach, pick up whatever's left that we can use, and move on."

7

"One thing for sure," Laurie Cole said as they stood amid the scattered remnants of their possessions and glanced ruefully about, "This fixes it so's I can't go east to that school. Everything I had is gone or destroyed—clothes, shoes—everything."

There was a note of relief, almost of joy, in the girl's voice. Morgan, poking about in a pile of papers with the toe of his boot, glanced up and shook his head angrily.

"No such a damn thing! You're still going. You can buy yourself new clothes when you get there."

"But how—"

"I don't want to hear about it. Pa said you had to go, and that's the way it'll be—and I aim to see that you do."

Laurie folded her arms across her breasts and considered her brother coolly. There was a stubborn glint in her eyes.

"It's not so much that you're determined to pack me off to that school as it is you're afraid to face Pa if I don't go."

Morgan's features were equally stubborn. "I'm doing what he told me to. Can't see anything wrong with that."

"Maybe not, but one of these days you'd better get

his foot off your neck and start doing for yourself. Pa won't live forever,'' Laurie stated and, turning to Temple, asked, ''What're we going to do now?''

''Start walking,'' he replied, ''and we best get at it. Still not sure whether those Apaches were up to something or not.''

He had probed about in the strewn wreckage for anything that would be useful and had come up with only the canteen of water Abe Valentine had kept under the seat of the stagecoach. The others in the party, having had baggage, also spent time searching about for anything of value or special meaning that the Indians might have overlooked. They found little.

''Which way we going?'' Ira Kelley asked when all were ready to move out.

''Doubtful Canyon'll be closer,'' Morgan Cole said before Temple could reply. ''All we've got to do is follow the road.''

''Way I see it, too,'' Temple said. ''No sense in going all the way back to Cottonwood.''

''Either way it'll be a hell of a walk,'' Kelley said, carefully adjusting the arm that was being supported by a sling. That his shoulder was paining him terribly was evident.

Clint Philbin grinned and scrubbed at his chin. ''Ain't you feeling good, Marshal? Them busted bones of yours bothering you some?''

''I'll make out,'' the lawman snapped. ''Don't you fret none about that.''

''Oh, I ain't fretting none,'' the outlaw countered. ''Things'll work out just fine for me.''

Kelley stared at his prisoner for a moment and then spat. ''If you're counting on them friends of yours to take you away from me, you'd best forget it. I'll be waiting—"

"Friends? What friends?" Philbin echoed mockingly. "Who said anything about me having friends coming to bust me loose?"

"That's what you're thinking," Kelley said, "and that's warning enough for me. . . . Come on, folks, let's climb back up to the road and get started."

Morgan Cole nodded his agreement and, reaching out for his sister, took her by the arm and pushed her toward the slope. Laurie jerked away and, lips set in a tight line, began to follow the lawman and his prisoner, already moving along the foot of the grade.

"Not sure it's smart to be up there on the road," Temple said, not moving.

Kelley paused "Why not? Be a damn sight easier walking—and somebody might just come along, a cowhand or maybe a pilgrim, that we could send for help "

"I was thinking about the Apaches Can bet they're keeping an eye on it—"

"They're gone. Said so yourself."

"That bunch is, but there's plenty others around. Those weren't the braves that jumped me—and probably wasn't the party that tried stopping the stage this morning. Country seems to be overrun with renegades right now."

"And they ain't supposed to be on the warpath," Gabriel muttered. "I'm siding with you, Temple I think we'd all better stay off the road and out of sight."

"Well, I ain't anxious to go stumbling along through a lot of brush and rocks," Philbin said. "I vote we do our walking on the road."

"You ain't got a vote," Kelley snarled. "Just you keep your lip buttoned—we'll do the deciding."

"Anybody know the country between here and Doubtful Canyon?" Temple asked. "Is there another town or maybe a ranch or homestead where we could get help?"

"There ain't nothing far as I recollect," Tom Gabriel said. "Made the trip a few times but was always on the road. I don't think there's anything in between, however."

"I've only been there once—Doubtful Canyon, I mean," Morgan Cole added. "Rode cross-country from the ranch. Never seen anything or anybody."

"Guess there's no chance of getting any help anywhere in between there and here then, so—"

"Come on, come on, let's head out!" Kelley broke in impatiently. "Was you that was worrying about them redskins coming back, so let's move!"

"You still aiming to take the road?"

The lawman nodded. "Walking it'll be bad enough. I sure ain't climbing my way over rocks and through the brush and cactus and up and down arroyos when I've got a choice. Besides, it'd take longer."

"Be the safest," Temple pointed out, convinced the lawman was making a mistake. "Up there in the open like we'd be, we wouldn't have a chance."

"That's how I see it," Gabriel said.

"Only one way to settle this," Morgan Cole declared. "The ones of us that figures it's better to go on the road will go that way. The others, meaning you and Temple, that thinks it's better to cut across country, why, then you go ahead and do it. We'll send back for you when we get to Doubtful Canyon."

The cattleman nodded agreement, but Temple was doubtful. "Not sure you people know what you're doing. It's not only that you have a lady with you, but you'll have only two guns, and one of them—the marshal—ain't in no shape to get in a fight.''

"We'll make out, mister!" Kelley said, aroused as well as out of patience. "Hell a'mighty man, you're overlooking the biggest thing! When this stage don't show up at Doubtful Canyon, the agent will be sending a party out to see what's wrong, and if we ain't up on the road, they won't be able to spot us.''

"There won't be anybody looking for us.'' Temple said quietly. "Abe Valentine told me this was a sort of an irregular run. Means the agent in Doubtful Canyon won't be expecting us at any particular time.''

The lawman's features clouded as he looked off across the low hills. Philbin swore. The information was not new to the Coles and Tom Gabriel, who appeared surprised at Kelley's ignorance of the fact.

"I reckon that'll change your thinking,'' Temple said.

The marshal brought his sharp glance back to the others. "Hell no, it don't change nothing! We're still better off up there where we can be seen if somebody comes along—and somebody's bound to. Now, I'm taking my prisoner and getting up there on the road and heading south. Rest of you do what you damn please I'm tired of arguing.''

Wheeling, the lawman, once more pushing Philbin into motion ahead of him, started along the base of the slope, looking for a break in the steep incline that would permit an ascent. Morgan Cole watched them briefly and then motioned to Laurie.

"Let's go—''

The girl hesitated and then, shrugging as if to say it meant little to her one way or the other, turned to do as her brother directed. Temple, taking the pistol that had

49

fallen from Valentine's boot, stepped forward and handed the weapon to her.

"Take this. You just might need it."

Laurie smiled and thrust the weapon under the waistband of her skirt. "I've got a feeling you're right."

"You'll need this, too," he added, placing the canteen of water in her hands.

The girl frowned. There was a small shine of perspiration on her cheeks and the tip of her nose, but she seemed not to notice. "But you—and Mr. Gabriel—you'll need—"

"We'll make out," Temple said.

Laurie's eyes softened. "You're very kind," she murmured, glancing at Morgan waiting impatiently nearby. "Good luck."

"Same to you," Temple said as the girl hurried off.

8

Gabriel, his eyes on Laurie's departing shape, smiled at Temple. "That's a fine little lady—and I've got a hunch she's sort of taken a shine to you."

"Wasting her time," Temple said flatly.

"Too bad. Feel kind of sorry for her, way that brother of hers bosses her around—and her pa, he must be a jim-dandy!"

"That's how it goes sometimes. Everything in this life can't be all sweetness and light."

The rancher smiled tightly and swiped at the sweat on his forehead. It was now well into midday, and the heat was making itself felt.

"You're right. Things sure can't always be just the way we want them to be."

Temple made no reply to that but said, "Time we was moving on, I expect. I think the smart thing to do is to follow the road, only stay a couple a hundred yards or so from it."

"Sounds good to me," the cattleman agreed as they struck off into the waist-high brush.

Overhead, vultures were already gathering, circling slowly as they centered on the dead horses lying near the wrecked stagecoach. There were no signs of the Apaches returning—nor was there any indication that

Ford Kailer and Amos Bell were anywhere in the area, all of which eased Temple's mind.

"Going to be a hot one—"

"Can bet on it," Temple replied absently.

The two men moved on, walking a steady but unhurried pace. The exact distance to Doubtful Canyon was not known to either, and although Tom Gabriel had made the journey from Cottonwood before, he could only say that they were in for a long walk.

"You're heading on west once we get to the way station, I remember hearing Lon Farley say—"

At Gabriel's words Temple shook his head. "May be that I'll change my mind about that and go down into Mexico instead."

"Mexico? What for?"

"Friend of mine's lined up with some Mexican general named Juarez, fighting the French. Said he could sort of fix me up with Juarez, too."

Gabriel, coat now off and slung across his shoulder, frowned as he shifted his bandaged arm which was now beginning to pain him.

"There's rumors that the French've pulled out and left it all to Benito Juarez."

"That so? Sure hadn't heard."

"Doubt if it'll hurt your chances any if it's true. Juarez still has his work cut out for him trying to pull everything together. Expect he'll be needing an army for some time to come."

"Obliged to you for telling me about it."

"Like I said, it's all a rumor, but my guess is that it's true. Whereabouts in Mexico were you told to go?"

"Chihuahua. Seems to be the headquarters for Juarez—or leastwise it was last time I heard from my friend. We were in the war together, and when it was over he went on down to Mexico and got into another one.''

"Expect Chihuahua's not the place any more, but I don't think you'll have any trouble locating Juarez. . . . You mentioned the war; you fought for the Union, I guess, judging from that hat you're wearing.''

Temple had shed his poncho and was carrying it at his side as they trudged on. "Was in the full four years, only I spent the last part of it in a Reb prison.''

"Never got into the fight myself. Had my ranch and my wife and two young ones on my hands. When it started, I gave it a lot of thought, finally decided I'd best stay with them. Tried to make up doing my part by selling my beef and some of my horses to the army, being a sort of supply depot for them.''

"Was just as important as carrying a musket. We were always needing grub and good horses.''

Gabriel hawked and spat. "Was the Confederate army I was supplying. My people were Tennesseans. I sort of leaned toward the South.''

John Temple was silent as they pressed on through the intense heat. He had seen no more of Marshal Kelley's party after separating and reckoned they had climbed to the road and were now well on their way to Doubtful Canyon. He hoped for their sake, but especially the girl's, that they would make it with no trouble. If luck was with them they would, but a deep-seated worry was gnawing at him and filling him with disturbing thoughts, and he wished now that he had insisted that Laurie and her brother stay with him and Gabriel.

The rancher's words registered on his consciousness. "Man has a right to his own beliefs and opinions.''

"Yeh, guess that's a fact. Where are you from?''

"Missouri—Bates County, over on the western side.'

"Kansas border."

"Right," Temple said in a suddenly taut sort o.
voice, "the Kansas border. You say you had a wife anc
two children?"

"All dead," Gabriel answered. "Fire. I don't know
what happened. I was out on the range one day looking
after part of the herd. Was winter, and we'd had a harc
snow. I was worried about the stock getting to feed.
When I got back to my place about dark, I found it
burnt to the ground with my wife and girls in it."

"Tough deal," Temple murmured sympathetically

"Can say that's the truth for sure. Hit me right then
while I was standing there waiting for the ashes to cool
that a man can work and struggle along to get somewhere,
and then one day something bad happens and his mind
kind of levels off and he asks himself: what the hell's
the use? And from then on he quits planning and scheming
and working for something better and starts living one
day at a time."

"I can understand that," Temple said but went no
further. "You got friends or relatives in Doubtful
Canyon?"

"No, got what you might say is a problem. Woman
there I'd like to marry—been kicking it around in my
head for quite a spell—but I ain't sure it's the thing to
do."

Temple glanced at the rancher. "Hell, man eithei
you want her for your wife or you don't. Sounds simple
enough to me."

"Not exactly the problem. I want her, all right, but it
bothers me what my relatives, especially the kin folks
of my dead wife, and my friends might think. You see

54

this woman works in a saloon in Doubtful Canyon. Everybody calls her Cinnamon because of her red hair. Real name is Lucy—Lucy Lovan."

"I can't see the problem—"

"Well, I'm not sure how my people will take to her, being a saloon girl and all that. Not that she's bad, because she sure ain't, but folks just sort of figure a woman who works in a saloon is a whore when that ain't always true. Plenty of them are widows who take the job to support themselves and maybe a couple of kids."

Temple slowed his step a bit and looked out over the heated rugged land to get his bearings. He didn't want to drift too far away from the road. Satisfied they were still on course, he turned back to the cattleman.

"The fact that she—Cinnamon—is working in a saloon—does that make a difference to you?"

"No, sure don't. I know she ain't pure as snow is white, same as I know she's been with other men—but then I don't figure I'm any bargain. Done a few things myself that would raise my folks' eyebrows, was they to know about it."

Temple shifted the poncho to his other arm, brushed his hat back, and wiped at the sweat on his forehead.

"Never was one to worry about what others think," he said indifferently.

"Always sort of felt that way myself, but Pastor Valley—that's where I've got my ranch—is a little place and real religious. Everybody knows everybody else and their business. If I bring Cinnamon there as my wife, I can figure on the whole town turning their backs on us."

Temple reached into his shirt pocket for one of the

stogies he'd purchased from Lon Farley in Cottonwood, withdrew instead a handful of crushed, shredded tobacco. Cursing, he threw the remnants of the cigars aside.

"Looks like a decision you'll have to make. Either you want the lady to be your wife and spend the rest of your days together, or you'll let what other folks think make you forget her."

"That's about the size of it," Gabriel said morosely. "It's come to where I've got to make a choice—and that'll be hard to do. Friends I'm talking about are good friends that I've known all my life. And my relatives and my wife's kinfolks—they stood by me during all my ups and downs. It's hell to go against them, just ignore what I know they'll think and feel."

"You can't fret over that—leastwise that's how I'd look at it. I'd figure it was my life and I had the right to lead it the way I wanted. If I made a mistake, it would be me that would pay for it—not any friend or kinfolk."

"You're saying I ought to go ahead, marry Cinnamon—and the hell with everybody else?"

"Just what I'm saying. It's your life. If you want to live it with her, it's your business."

Tom Gabriel nodded solemnly as, hat pulled low over his eyes to shield them from the glaring sunlight, they pushed on. Off to their left a covey of startled quail suddenly exploded into the motionless, hot air, the thunder of their departure momentarily breaking the breathless silence that gripped the land.

"Couple of them roasted would sure taste good right now," the rancher observed absently. Then, "Not sure doing what you say would be all that easy. Be like just cutting away half your life, putting it behind you, and starting all over."

56

"Could be that's just what you're needing—a fresh start."

Gabriel slanted a look at Temple. "That what you're doing? You leaving some of your life behind and hunting for a new life in Mexico?"

At the pointed implication Temple only shrugged, admitting nothing, denying nothing. The cattleman again swiped at the sweat on his face.

"Didn't mean to get nosy—was just trying to square things about in my head," he said apologetically.

"Forget it," Temple replied and again let the matter drop.

Crossing the border into Mexico was all important to him for the very reasons vaguely hinted at by Tom Gabriel, but it was not a matter for discussion. It had been easy, and quick, to become an outlaw, just as it now would be most difficult, perhaps impossible, to turn back and become a law-abiding citizen.

It was all in the cards fate dealt a man, just as a hero is never born but becomes such through circumstances. Throughout his life Temple had honored the law, respecting and living by it. And then within the space of only seconds, thanks to Union Army General Thomas Ewing's ill-conceived plan known generally as Order Number Eleven, he had become an outlaw. It was to be expected. Any man living by his conscience instinctively does what he believes is right without thought of possible consequences if he is to find peace within himself.

"You best do your own figuring," Temple said. "I'm no big shucks when it comes to handing out advice and telling folks what they ought to do—only know what I'd do was it me. It's up to you—"

A not too distant crackle of gunshots cut into John

Temple's words. Turned silent abruptly, he drew up stiffly and listened. Again there was a flurry of reports, hollow and flat in the afternoon heat.

"That's coming from the road!" he said in a tight voice. "Means the Cole girl and the others are in trouble. We'd better get there fast!"

9

Immediately John Temple broke into a hard, loping run to the source of the gunshots—a quarter mile or so ahead, he judged. Gabriel, holding his wounded arm with a free hand to prevent its being jostled, followed close.

The shooting continued, at first sparingly but then in a steady, spaced roll. Shortly Temple and the rancher could hear the yelling of the Indians, and, sucking deep for breath, they increased their pace. But running through the clinging brush with stretches of loose sand periodically underfoot made speed not only difficult but doubly tiring, and by the time the two men were near enough to see the renegade Apaches racing back and forth on their horses, both were gasping for wind.

"Got—to—hold off—a bit," Gabriel said, sinking onto a rock. Head slung forward, flushed face tipped down as he struggled to fill his heaving lungs, he added, "I couldn't—do no good now—shape I'm in."

Temple, equally sweat soaked, felt much the same and, dropping to his knees nearby, fixed his attention on the road above—some hundred feet or so distant. Through the screen of plume and rabbit brush and occasional mesquite, he caught fleeting glimpses of the Indians as they whipped about, some shooting with rifles, others making use of bows and arrows. He could not see the Coles and the rest of the party but guessed they had found refuge of some kind that was enabling them to hold off the renegades.

As Temple watched, one of the braves abruptly doubled forward over the neck of his pony and fell to the ground, his coppery body bouncing slackly when it struck the hard surface.

At that the yelling heightened. Temple came to his feet quickly. He and Gabriel could delay no longer.

"We better get up there," he said and, not waiting for the rancher, began to claw his way up the slope in a slanting course.

Gabriel was close behind, and by the time Temple had gained the edge of the road and was crouched behind a clump of gray-green desert broom, the cattleman, despite his injured arm, had caught up and was at his side.

The Coles with Marshal Kelley and his prisoner had taken shelter in a pile of large boulders, which had dislodged at some time during one of the wild rainstorms that infrequently lashed the country and tumbled down from the higher regions of the mountain along which the road followed.

It was not possible to see if any of the party had been wounded or not, but they were managing to maintain a line of fire that was forcing the Apaches to keep their distance. Only one of the renegades had been killed, however.

"Near a dozen of them," he said, making a quick count. "We've got to make them think there's more than two of us."

Gabriel nodded agreement but frowned. "Don't see just how—"

"We'll keep below the edge of the road and move about. Every time we shoot, we'll move—go ten or twelve feet from where we were—then shoot again. Maybe we can fool them into thinking there's several of us."

"Ought to work," Gabriel said and, pistol in hand, began to work his way along the grade.

When he was a distance from Temple, he raised the hand in which he held his weapon and signaled that he was ready. At once Temple crawled close to the lip of the road's shoulder and, masked by rocks and bunch grass, leveled his pistol at the nearest of the braves riding straight for the rocks where the Coles and the lawman and his prisoner were. The Apache, not a young man but showing some age, was yelling wildly as he pointed the Sharps rifle he was carrying at the beleaguered party.

Waiting until he was certain of his aim, Temple triggered his pistol. The brave fell from his horse instantly, cut down by a bullet in the head. Several of the warriors, abruptly aware of the shot, wheeled, began to move toward what they believed to be the source of the bullet. In that moment Tom Gabriel fired his weapon, dropping a second brave.

Taking advantage of the distraction, Temple hurriedly moved more to his left. The braves by then were milling uncertainly about in the drifting dust and smoke. In his new location Temple fired again, but the brave moved, and the bullet missed its intended target and buried itself instead in the Apache's shoulder.

At almost the same instant Cole, or perhaps it was

Marshal Ira Kelley, triggered his weapon and another of the renegades sagged on his pony and fell to the road. Immediately Gabriel, now also in a different position along the slope, fired twice in quick succession. One of the bullets went wide, struck a rock on the hillside beyond, and caromed off into space with a shrill screeching; the other burned across the hindquarters of a brave's pony and set it to pitching wildly about on the narrow roadway.

That proved to be enough for the renegades. One of them yelled, waved his rifle above his head, and, drumming heels against the ribs of his mount, rushed off in the direction of a distant group of trees. His companions, losing no time, sunlight glistening off their sweaty skins, followed instantly.

At once Temple scrambled to his feet and made it to the crest of the slope. "The horses—Cole!" he shouted. "Grab one—"

Not hesitating, Temple holstered his gun and started for one of the two animals standing in the center of the roadway. Cole, now upright at the edge of the rocks where he had been doing his shooting, seemed momentarily confused.

"The horses!" Temple shouted again. "Get one of them!"

Morgan Cole was nearest to the ponies, and at once he moved hurriedly toward them. Suddenly there was a jingle of metal and the sound of scuffling somewhere behind him as Marshal Kelley experienced difficulty of some sort in forcing his prisoner to comply with demands.

The disturbance was too much for the already skittish horses. They came about in a swirl of dust and, tails up, pounded off down the road in pursuit of the Indian party, now little more than a blur of color on the flat to the east.

Temple swore under his breath. "We needed one of those broomtails," he said in a bitter voice. "Could've sent somebody to the way station for help on it."

Morgan Cole lifted his hands and let them fall to his sides in a gesture of despair. "Was about to get a hold on the gray when the marshal spooked him."

Kelley, shoving the manacled Clint Philbin out of the rocks ahead of him, cursed angrily. On beyond them Laurie appeared and, hurrying by, literally threw herself upon John Temple.

"I'm—I'm so glad you got here! I've never been so scared in my life!"

Morgan Cole drew up stiffly, folded his arms across his chest and, frowning, stared at his sister. Temple, a bit taken aback, gently disengaged Laurie's arms and stepped away.

"Same here," he mumbled, unable to think of anything else to day.

"Can tell you this," Ira Kelley said, "you two got here just in time! We was starting to run low on ammunition. With only two of us doing the shooting, it was taking plenty of lead."

Tom Gabriel moved up to Laurie. He was holding his wounded arm stiffly before him, and from the bits of leaves and dirt clinging to his coat sleeve it would appear that he had fallen sometime during the encounter with the Apaches.

"Can you spare me a bit of that water?" he asked in his slow, polite way.

Immediately the girl passed the canteen to the rancher who took a quick swallow and then handed the container

63

to Temple Mindful of the long, hot miles that apparently still lay before them, he also allowed himself but a small amount, barely enough, in fact, to wet his throat.

"Well I best say it now," Ira Kelley declared, mopping at his face and neck with a bandanna. Either he was ignoring the pain in his broken shoulder or it had reached the stage of total numbness, for his rugged, lined features were reflecting no signs of discomfort. "You was right and I was dead wrong. We should've stayed clear of this here damned road. Them savages was just setting up here waiting for us to come along, just like you figured."

"We barely made it to them rocks before they was on us," Clint Philbin volunteered.

Temple turned to the edge of the slope and retrieved his poncho, abandoned during the shooting. "Nobody got hurt—that's the important thing," he said, looking off across the ragged, broken country to the south. "Expect we'd better keep on moving through the brush and sticking to low ground. Could be another bunch hanging around."

"I don't doubt that one whit," the lawman said. "Just you lead off. Far as I'm concerned, you're the head man from here on."

Temple nodded and crossed to the nearest of the dead Apaches. Disappointment rolled through him when he rolled the brave over. He had only a bow and a quiver of arrows. Temple had hoped for a rifle with a supply of ammunition. The other warriors proved also to be armed with primitive weapons—one with a short lance, the others with bows and obsidian-tipped feathered shafts.

"Seems we drew a low card all the way around far as that bunch of redskins are concerned," Tom Gabriel murmured at his side. "Missed out on horses and weapons both."

Temple shrugged. "Horses would have sure helped a'plenty. Same goes for a rifle or two, but we didn't have any luck with either, so there's no use talking about it."

He felt fingers touch his wrist and turned to face Laurie Cole.

"I've still got that pistol you gave me," she said. "It's empty—I used up all the bullets shooting at those Indians. If you have more—"

Taking the weapon from her, Temple glanced about at the men. "Bullets I've got won't work—it's a forty-four cap-and-ball. Any of you help?"

Ira Kelley said, "Nope, not my caliber either."

"Same here," Gabriel added. "I'm using the new style cartridge."

"Goes for me too," Morgan Cole stated, completing the roll, and looked down at Laurie. "Looks like you'll just have to forget that gun, little sister."

The girl sniffed. "Were you afraid that I might use it to get away from you?"

"Could be," Morgan replied with a crooked smile. "But six-shooter or not, you ain't about to do that."

It was Laurie's turn to smile. "Don't bet on it," she said and taking the weapon from Temple thrust it back under the waistband of her skirt.

Temple watched the angry flush rise in Morgan Cole's neck and spread to his cheeks and waited for the man to make a reply of some sort. When it did not come, he turned to Gabriel. "That arm bothering you much?"

"Some," the rancher admitted, "but I'll make out."

"How about your shoulder?" Temple continued, shifting his attention to Ira Kelley.

"Don't worry none about me," the lawman replied gruffly. "Let's just get moving."

"Fine with me," Temple said and, pivoting, started down the slope for the flat below.

10

Reaching the foot of the grade, Temple paused briefly to make certain of directions and then struck off through the brush. He was slightly in the lead but shortly found Laurie Cole at his shoulder. Glancing about, Gabriel, a few steps to the left, caught his eye and grinned. Morgan Cole, scowling his disapproval of his sister's actions, was next to the rancher while a distance behind the outlaw Clint Philbin and the marshal brought up the rear.

The afternoon sun, now out full strength in a cloudless sky, struck at them from the side as they bore steadily southward, and within less than a quarter hour each member of the struggling party was wet with sweat.

The ground itself made walking most difficult. There was no arroyo furrowing off into the right direction in which a sandy floor would provide a smooth if somewhat loose surface upon which to travel, but instead they were faced with uneven, broken land, studded with sharp-edged black lava rock, slashed by ragged gullies, and covered by low-growing chaparral, clawing cactus, and needle-pointed yucca that stabbed at their legs.

There appeared to be no animal life anywhere. The heaven above was devoid of birds, the country about them lay hushed beneath the intense heat with no signs

of coyotes, prairie dogs, rabbits, or any other anima
that a man could expect to see. Even the raucous insect
were not to be heard.

There was something foreboding about it all, John
Temple thought; a sort of warning seemed to be hanging
in the air, but of what he could not fathom. The sky was
empty and gave no hint of a storm—and it couldn't get
much hotter.

He cast a side glance at Laurie. To simplify walking
she had converted her dress into makeshift trousers by
drawing it up between her legs and tucking the back
hem into the waistband. Her shoes, however, were
something else. Soft and lightweight, they would not
long withstand the harsh treatment they were being
subjected to. Her jacket was off and was now a crumpled
roll in one hand, while the scarf that covered her dark
hair had been pulled forward to shade her eyes.

As Temple watched, Laurie staggered slightly. He
caught the girl by her arm, steadied her, and looked
ahead. A solitary stunted scrub oak made a green globular
silhouette in a sink off to their left. At once he altered
course for it.

"There's a bit of shade coming up," he said. "Can
rest a bit—and it looks like we're getting out of this
lava bed. Walking won't be so hard."

Laurie nodded gratefully and managed a weak smile.
Shortly the party reached the hollow, and all immediately
found a place in the meager shade being cast by the oak
and sank down onto the hot red soil to take what ease
they could.

"Could sure have used one of them redskins' ponies,"
Ira Kelley said, gently stroking his injured shoulder
"You should've caught one of them, boy," he added

accusingly, settling his glance on Morgan. "Yes, sir, you sure should've."

Cole, features red from the heat, clothing dark and plastered to his body with sweat, swore angrily.

"Should've—hell! I just about had one when you had to go slam-banging around in the rocks with that prisoner of yours!"

"Was giving me sass," the lawman said calmly. "And I ain't about to take any off him—or you—or anybody else. And if you—"

"Ease off," Temple cut in. "We're all on edge. No use making things worse by snapping at each other. Having to put up with this heat's plenty for all of us."

"Well, he should've caught that black horse," Laurie said, coming into the conversation. "If it had been Pa telling him to, you can bet he would have—even if he had to chase the damn thing on foot for a mile!"

Morgan stiffened. "Be enough of that kind of talk!"

"No, it won't be enough!" the girl continued. "I'm tired of you pussyfooting around, spying on me—and trying to run my life like he does yours!"

"If you're meaning by that me keeping you from tying up with that no account Harley Edge, then I'll admit it. I agree with Pa there—and I ain't going to let you throw yourself away on—"

"There's nothing wrong with Harley except he's poor! One thing for sure—and what you don't like about him—is that he's a man. He stands on his own two feet, and that's more than you can say—"

"Damn it—you shut your mouth!" Morgan shouted, lunging toward the girl with arm raised and hand open to deliver a slap. "I'll—"

Temple reached out quickly, seized Cole by the slack in his shirt, and pulled him back. "Cool off, Morgan."

69

Cole jerked free of Temple's restraining fingers. "Stay out of this!" he snarled. "It's none of your butt-in!"

"I'll stay out of it up to the point where you start slapping her around," Temple said coldly "I won' stand for that."

Morgan Cole settled down and brushed at his face with a bandanna. The hush held in the shallow sink for several minutes, and then he shrugged. "I do what Pa tells me to, Laurie, because I work for him—and part of the job is looking after you. If you had a lick of sense you'd see that all he wants is the best for you—"

"Ha!" Laurie said with fine scorn. "That's not it—he's set his mind on making me do what he wants! Pa doesn't give a hoot about what I want. It's my life and I—"

"And you're fool enough to throw it away on Harley Edge if we don't stop you. You don't love him, Laurie Only reason you're stuck on him is that you think he's a means for getting away from Pa."

"That's not true!" the girl shouted, starting to rise. "I—"

Temple, weary of the quarrel, motioned her back down. She was panting from anger, and color was high in her cheeks.

"Too hot for all that," he said quietly. "And you'd both better save your strength for what's ahead. We've got a far piece to go, I expect."

Morgan Cole shook his head wearily. "Always like this—pure hell all the time just because she can't have her way. If I had the say-so, I'd let her go—let Harley Edge have her. Sure would be a load off my shoulders."

"You can shed it anytime," Laurie shot back caustically. "It's certainly not me that's asking you to bear it."

"I'll be shed of it tomorrow when I put you on that stage for St. Louis—"

"I'm not on it yet—and even if I do board it, you won't be along to keep me from getting off somewhere—"

"Pa—we've got that all taken care of, so you can just forget it. I've got the money to pay the driver and the shotgun to see that you don't get off until—"

"They can't keep an eye on me every minute!"

Morgan smiled tightly. "When you've got the money, you can get anything done you want—and that's what I aim to do—pay to see that you're delivered to that school Pa picked out for you."

Laurie was silent after that and, lying back in the mottled shadow of the oak, stared up into the barren sky. After a time she turned her head slightly and put her eyes on John Temple, considered his hard-cornered browned features thoughtfully.

"Do you have any sisters, Temple?" she asked

"Yes—had two."

"Had?"

"They're dead," he replied bluntly and, getting to his feet, walked to the edge of the shade.

"I'm sorry," Laurie murmured and, rising, followed him. "I didn't mean to open old sores—"

"Forget it. It's all in the past."

"I wish all this was in the past—that we had reached Doubtful Canyon, that I'd met Harley—or somebody— and was on my way to a new life—and had only tomorrow to think about."

Temple was quiet for a long breath and then, "Can't plan too much on tomorrows—nobody can promise them to you for certain. A lot of things can happen."

.Laurie was standing beside him, so near that her shoulder touched his own. "I know that, and I don't expect things to be just right for me all the time. But I want to live my own life. Don't I have a right to do that?"

"Everybody has that right, but it could be your pa just wants the best for you."

"That's it exactly! *He wants!* Nobody seems interested in what I want. If you had a daughter, wouldn't you hope for her to be happy, not just have her do what you thought she ought to?"

"Reckon I'd want the best for her, and that would be whatever made her happy."

"You'd want her to be happy—that's what I'm talking about!"

Temple shrugged, irritated at having been drawn into a family controversy. Coming about, he glanced at the others in the party. All appeared rested and somewhat cooler for their rest in the sink.

"Time we moved on," he said.

Tom Gabriel drew himself wearily upright. Morgan Cole, his features sharply suspicious as his glance touched Temple, followed. Clint Philbin did not move when Kelley rose but remained sprawled in the shadow of the oak. The lawman, pistol in hand, regarded him coldly for a moment or two and then, drawing back his booted foot, kicked the outlaw soundly in the ribs.

Philbin yelped, rolled over, and got to his feet. "Damn you—you old sonofabitch! I'll get back at you for this—wait and see!"

"Watch your mouth," the lawman snapped. "I don't like being called that by any man. And far as getting back at me, you'll never see that day!"

"That's maybe what you think, grandpa," Philbin said with a smirk. "Could be you've got a surprise coming."

"Ain't likely," Kelley said mildly, again holding the arm of his injured shoulder in an effort to ease the pain. "But I'll be ready for it."

11

They moved on in the blistering heat. No breeze drifted down from the low-lying mountains to the east bringing relief, and the brazen sky was a cauldron that offered no break in the soaring temperature.

"How—how far is it to the way station?" Laurie asked in a dragging voice. "Does anybody know?"

Temple halted and turned to Gabriel for the answer. The rancher, swiping at the sweat on his forehead, glanced about as if searching for familiar landmarks. They were presently following a low embankment that ran parallel to the road, some half-mile or so now to the west. Heavy brush, mostly mesquite and chaparral, covered the land, and traveling had been slow and difficult.

"Ain't sure," Gabriel said. "I'm just not remembering any of this, but my guess would be that we've still got about thirty miles to go."

Laurie sighed deeply. Ira Kelley wagged his head in a gesture of weariness intensified by pain, and Philbin cursed softly.

"This is one hell of a note," he declared. "Got me all cuffed and walking and knuckling under to this beat-up old man. For crissake, turn me loose! I've got a feeling we ain't ever going to make it to that way station, so I'm asking you to make these irons off me so's I can at least try to get somewhere on my own!''

"We'll make it," Kelley said doggedly. "You just keep your mouth shut and save your breath. Far as turning you loose—that ain't never going to happen Never! No matter what!''

Philbin spat. "Expect I'll be alive and kicking a long time after you're dead and buried, grandpa!'' Philbin shot back. "Can save yourself a heap of trouble by doing what I asked.''

Kelley's small black eyes glittered. "It'll be snowing in hell the day I turn you loose, killer!''

Temple glanced about at the people gathered before him. An ironic smile parted his dry, cracked lips. He was a hell of a long way from Mexico, and what had started out as a race to get there before serious trouble overtook him had devolved into his becoming caretaker for a headstrong girl seeking to escape the will of a dominating father, her brother laboring also under the heavy hand of their parent while striving anxiously to fulfill the tasks assigned him.

Add to them a love-struck, wounded rancher torn between the woman he wanted and the opinions of friends and relatives; an aged lawman, also wounded, determined to deliver his prisoner, whom he hated with a fiery passion, to a higher authority; and the outlaw himself, who apparently entertained hopes of being rescued from the law by friends whom he believed would be waiting somewhere ahead.

He'd be mighty lucky if he ever saw Mexico, John Temple thought wryly! And if Ford Kailer and Amos Bell had managed to escape the Apaches back there on the flats west of Cottonwood, they could just be closing in again on him, which would further reduce his chances of seeing Mexico.

Shifting about, Temple stared off in the direction of the road. The two men could actually be somewhere along its dusty length at that very moment—heading for Doubtful Canyon. If so, he could expect them to be there awaiting him when, and if, he made it through.

Such had deeper meaning, he realized. The pair would reach the way station expecting to find the stage from Cottonwood there ahead of them. When it became known that it had not arrived, the station agent would immediately conclude that the coach had run into trouble and dispatch a search party. For that reason it became apparent to Temple that he should return to the road.

But there was no assurance that such was the case. Kailer and Bell might never have reached Cottonwood; but if they had, and later enroute to Doubtful Canyon spotted the wrecked Celerity at the bottom of the slope, they could have turned back upon finding no survivors and given up the chase.

Temple swore softly as his shoulders stirred in a gesture of frustration. It was impossible to know exactly what had happened. He could only keep on as he was and do the best he could to get the people with him and himself safely to the stagecoach way station somewhere— no one knew just how far—ahead.

"How about a swig of that there water?"

Clint Philbin's harsh voice brought an end to Temple's thoughts.

"Go easy," he heard Gabriel, who had taken charge of the canteen, say. "Good chance it'll have to last us till we get to where we're going."

The outlaw tipped the container to his lips and began

to swallow greedily. Immediately the cattleman snatched it away. Philbin grinned and wiped his mouth.

"Ain't going to make no difference. If the Indians don't get us, this here desert will. And while we're talking, I'm getting powerful hungry," he added, turning to Ira Kelley. "You're supposed to feed a prisoner, old man. Why ain't you out rustling up a rabbit or two?"

They were all hungry, Temple knew, and with water running low in the canteen, there was a good chance they'd also be very thirsty before the way station was reached.

"How about it, Mister Lawman?" Philbin continued in his irritating nasal voice. "You going to get me something to eat?"

"You'll eat when the rest of us do," the marshal replied wearily.

"Well, that ain't good enough for me!" the outlaw stated angrily. "I'm going to set myself down right here, and I ain't moving till you scare up something to eat."

Temple, impatience building slowly within him, watched as Philbin settled himself on the ground. Nearby Morgan Cole, Laurie, and Tom Gabriel looked on.

"Get up," Kelley ordered, shifting his pistol to his left hand while he reached down with the right and grasped the outlaw by the collar of his shirt.

Philbin rocked to one side, jerked free, and made a grab for the marshal's weapon. His fingers wrapped about the barrel of the pistol, and with a yank he took it from the lawman.

"Now—damn you," he began as he rolled to his feet. "We'll see just who's running this show. Soon as I get these cuffs off me—"

Clint Philbin never got to finish his threat. Temple in

a single swift stride was upon him. His balled fist lashed out. There was a sharp crack as it caught the outlaw on the jaw. Philbin grunted, staggered back, and dropped onto a clump of brush, losing his grip on the pistol as he did.

Still simmering, Temple retrieved the weapon and handed it to Kelley, who muttered an unintelligible thanks. Pride was having its way with Ira Kelley in those moments; he was doubtless finding it hard to accept the fact that he had reached a time in life when he was no longer fully capable of handling a prisoner.

"Damned arm of mine," he mumbled. "Just can't seem to get a'hold of things right."

Philbin stirred and sat up. Touching the lawman with a hateful look, he switched his agate-hard eyes to Temple.

"You're going to be mighty damn sorry you horned in, mister!" he said, rubbing his jaw as best he could with a manacled hand. "I ain't forgetting this!"

"You figuring to get even from the grave after they string you up?" Temple asked dryly.

"I'm a long way from that—"

"Which means you'll make your try if and when those friends you're banking on bust you loose—"

The expression on Clint Philbin's sweaty, whisker-stubbled face broke slightly with surprise. "Friends? I don't know nothing about no friends!"

Temple smiled, turned, and glanced at the others in the party. Worn, clothing marked with dark splotches where sweat had soaked through, lips cracked, eyes red-rimmed, and bodies sagging with fatigue, they were in poor condition to continue. But they could not remain there.

"Best we move out—"

Laurie, walking beside Gabriel as if to garner a measure

78

of strength from him, started forward. Morgan Cole was a step behind.

Ira Kelley, apparently suffering much from the rough handling he'd received from Philbin, prodded the outlaw with the toe of his boot.

"Get up—we're going on."

"The hell with it! I'm staying right here."

"I reckon not," Temple said quietly and, stepping past the lawman, caught the outlaw by an arm and yanked him to his feet.

"Move out!" he snarled, giving the man a hard shove.

Philbin, cursing wildly, stumbled forward, caught himself, and wheeled to face Temple. "Telling you again, I ain't forgetting how you slapped me around—'

Anger, weariness, frustration—all intensified by the extreme heat in a situation where all things seemed to be going against him—sent John Temple's temper to the boiling point. Head thrust forward, big fists knotted, and blazing eyes narrowed, he took a step toward Philbin.

"Never you mind," Ira Kelley said, injecting himself in between the two men. "Ain't no call for you to take a hand in bringing in my prisoner. I can do it."

"Then, by God, see that you do!" Temple said, halting. "I'm damn sick of him holding us back!" Pivoting stiffly, he moved on to catch up with the others.

They pushed on through the waning afternoon with the slowly lowering sun still bearing down intensely on them. Several times Temple called a stop to rest in the scant filagree shade of a mesquite or desert broom when it appeared that Laurie Cole was near to collapse

Gabriel, too, was now in a bad way from the wound in his arm, as was Marshal Kelley whose shoulder pained him constantly. Only Morgan, Clint Philbin, and he seemed to be weathering the ordeal, but just how much longer any of them could continue under the conditions that beset them was a guess. They would have to have food and additional water soon; Temple doubted they could make it through the next day without either

Moving off to one side, Temple climbed to a mound that rose a dozen feet or so above the flat. There was no change in the land as near as he could tell—just the long running prairie with the bluff-like wall to the north, the endless miles of brush, some of it shoulder high, extending on and on indefinitely. And then through the shimmering heat hovering over the land, he thought he saw a change and catching Tom Gabriel's eye beckoned to him.

Pointing to what appeared to be a faint line of green in the far distance, he said "That look like—"

"Trees—surer'n hell!' the rancher exclaimed before Temple could finish "Growing along a creek—or maybe a river!'

Temple nodded agreement, and as they turned to rejoin the others said, "Ought to reach it by dark, maybe a bit after, if we move right along."

"Won't be no trouble doing that soon as we tell them about it," Gabriel said "Looks like we'll be set for the night, at least."

"Reckon so,' Temple replied "Can let tomorrow take care of itself "

12

It was Morgan Cole who caught the glint of water tracing along the green band and called it to everyone's attention.

"It's a creek!" he shouted hoarsely.

Temple and Gabriel exchanged glances. They had decided earlier to say nothing about it as there was always the possibility that a stream or spring would be dry at that time of year.

But there definitely was water, and, spirits revived, the party pressed on through the fading day; and shortly before the sun disappeared behind the mountains well to the west, they reached the oasis—a narrow winding stand of brush, willows, and small cottonwood trees crowding a shallow stream barely the width of a wagon bed.

"Let's go in easy," Temple cautioned. "Don't want to walk in on that bunch of Apaches."

"Just could be here all right," Gabriel agreed.

The warning halted a rush to the water, and all, including Clint Philbin, proceeded quietly. They arrived at the creek and, as one, sank down on their knees beside it to first satisfy their thirst and then revel in the coolness that came with bathing their faces and necks and lowering their heads into the stream.

Temple, not thoroughly convinced that no Apaches were in the area, indulged himself briefly and then, moving on beyond his party, sought out higher ground. There he turned his attention to all directions, listening for any sounds that would indicate the presence of the renegade braves and sniffing the air for the odor of smoke. When he could find nothing to disturb him, he returned to the camp to find the members of the group stretched out along the banks of the creek taking their ease.

"You going to rustle us up something to eat?" Philbin greeted, ignoring Ira Kelley, who appeared to be suffering intensely, and directing his question to Temple. "This here creek's a waterhole for all kinds of varmints. Bound to be something you can catch and roast. . . . Now, if you don't think you can, get the key off the marshal there and take off these cuffs, and I'll do it."

"Apaches make use of this water, too—can bet on it," Temple replied. "I couldn't turn up any signs of them, but I don't figure that's any guarantee they're not around. Building a fire would be the same as inviting them to jump us."

A small sound of disappointment slipped from Laurie Cole's throat. She brushed at her eyes wearily. "I—I'm so hungry. I forgot to eat before we left home. I thought we would be at the way station by now, and—"

The girl's voice trailed off into nothing. Clint Philbin sat up and glared at Temple. "You see there! I ain't the only one needing something to eat! You got to—"

"He don't have to do nothing for you," Kelley, rousing, broke in. "Settle back there and shut up. We'll do what we can."

"Sure don't want to bring them Apaches down on us," Morgan Cole said, glancing about. "And there ain't nothing around here we can find that won't need cooking.''

"Ought to be some berry bushes growing along the stream," Temple said. "Let's split up and see what we can find before it gets too dark; but go quiet—and don't get too far from camp.''

Laurie and Morgan rose and immediately began to make their way along the banks of the creek, one on either side. Temple nodded to Kelley.

"Stay with your prisoner, Marshal. Gabriel and me will see what we can come up with," he said and moved off with the rancher, separating as did the Coles but starting off in the opposite direction taken by them.

A hundred yards or so later they came upon a cluster of gooseberry bushes and at once began to fill their hats with the still somewhat green berries.

"Seems there should be some wild onions along here too," Gabriel remarked when they started back to camp. "Too dark to go looking for some now, but we could in the morning.''

The Coles had not returned when Temple and the cattleman reached the small clearing alongside the stream where they had halted. The two men divided their take of berries with the lawman and his prisoner, who at once complained that they were far from ripe and not fit to eat. Temple closed his ears to the man's griping and began to worry a bit about Laurie and Morgan, wondering if they had become lost or encountered trouble. He was about to set out in search of the pair when they appeared. They not only had found berry bushes but had come upon a patch of wild onions as well and brought a large supply with them.

It wasn't much of a meal—half-ripe gooseberries and wild onions—but it took the edge off their hunger, and now with a wealth of water nearby and the heat of the day fading as night closed in, all settled back to make the best of their situation.

"Going to get cold tonight," Tom Gabriel commented, glancing up at the sky. It had a clean, swept look in the last reflected rays of the sun. "Got a feeling the wind's going to blow too."

"Something we can do without," Temple said laconically. Then, "We'll need to set up a watch. Don't want any Apaches surprising us."

"Just what I was thinking," the rancher said. "Can divide it between you, Cole, and me. . . . I'm not sleepy. I'll take the first stretch."

Temple, dead on his feet, nevertheless shook his head. "How about your arm? You sure you're up to it?"

The cattleman grinned. "It's hurting plenty, but that'll keep me awake."

"Won't argue with you. Seems like a month since I laid down and shut my eyes. Give me a couple of hours and then wake me."

"I'll make it three. That will split it up even."

The wind was rising steadily when Gabriel woke John Temple. Refreshed by even so short a period of rest, he crossed at once to the pocket of brush at the edge of the camp where it was possible to have a good view not only of the sleeping members of the party huddled together against the cold but also of the approaches to the clearing as well.

There had been no suspicious sounds during his watch, the rancher had said, but he had seen three coyotes and several small animals come into the creek for water.

A groan from Marshal Kelley drew Temple's attention

as he was preparing to assume his post on the rock Gabriel had managed to roll into place for a seat, and, moving to the old lawman's side, he knelt over him Kelley appeared feverish and no doubt was suffering greatly from his shoulder. But there was nothing that could be done for the man until they reached Doubtful Canyon where, hopefully, a doctor would be available.

"What'll it take to get you to turn me loose?"

The cautiously voiced question came from Clint Philbin a stride or two beyond the marshal. Looking closely, Temple saw that Kelley, probably with the aid of either Cole or Gabriel, had compelled the outlaw to put his arms around one of the small cottonwoods and then locked his wrists together again with the handcuffs.

"I'm meaning—how much cash—gold?"

"Wasting your breath," Temple said and, pivoting, returned to his station in the brush.

Seating himself on the rock, he drew the poncho he was wearing more closely about him wishing at the moment that he had his heavy wool brush coat. But it had been lost with the rest of the gear left on his horse lying dead on the flats near Cottonwood. Likely some Apache was enjoying its warmth at that very moment.

One among the sleeping members of the party stirred and sat up. Watching, Temple saw that it was the girl. She drew herself to her feet and, arms clasped tightly to her slender body in an effort to ward off the cold, hurried toward him.

"I'm freezing!" she chattered as she halted. "Can I sit here close to you?"

Temple made room on the rock for her, and then taking the poncho he opened it lengthwise and draped it about both their shoulders. Immediately she snuggled in close.

"Thank you," she murmured. "I'm beginning to feel warmer already."

Temple resumed his steady surveillance of the camp and the area around it, conscious all the while of Laurie's body pressing against him.

"Have you got a wife somewhere, Temple?"

At her question he shook his head. "No, sure haven't."

"Hard to believe some woman wouldn't have grabbed you a long time ago. You're nice looking and you have a strong way about you that a girl likes '

Temple stirred self-consciously. No woman had ever said such things to him before, and to hear them now from a young and pretty girl like Laurie Cole filled him with a mixture of pride and embarrassment.

He glanced at the sky. It was a dark canopy strewn with glittering stars, dominated by a moon that looked as if i were made of ice. The wind was continuing to increase in strength, and now the tops of the trees were beginning to whip back and forth vigorously while a low whistling sound was building in the brush. The night would become a wild one before it was over, he reckoned, but hoped it would blow itself out by daylight.

"Would you marry me, Temple?"

He drew up in surprise. "Now, what makes you ask a question like that? You know that we've just met— that I don't mean anything to you and—well—you don't love me like two people should if they're to marry."

"Maybe I do. I've been with you now for most of a day and night, and I've really come to like you—more than just like you, in fact. I've heard that people can fall in love at first sight. I think I have—"

"No, I don't think so," Temple said quietly. "Could be you're trying to make yourself believe it, but what you're doing is looking for a way to get out from under your pa's thumb.''

Laurie was silent for a time. Then, ''I guess that is part of it or, at least, that's what started it all. I was ready to do anything that would take me away from him.''

''Sort of figured that from what you and your brother said back there a piece—''

''Oh, Morgan! He's just like Pa, and he'll do anything Pa tells him to—jump off a cliff—whatever! Can't you see, Temple, that's why I have to leave and get off on my own. I won't let myself become another Morgan.''

''You sure your pa's not right in wanting something better for you than just being the wife of some cowhand? That's a mighty hard life.''

Laurie listened to the whistling of the wind for several moments. Snuggling even closer to Temple, she said, ''Maybe so, but at least it would be a life of my own choosing. Pa's been telling me for years that he wanted me to grow up to be a lady, not a female cowhand—''

''I reckon I can understand that.''

''Perhaps, but I can't, and won't, because I don't give a hoot about being a lady I'm going to pick my own kind of life—one with somebody like you, Temple. . . . Why couldn't we make it together—why couldn't you take me with you? I know I could make you happy if you'd give me a chance '

Temple stared off into the blustery night, filled now with the sound of the wind which had risen to a shriek

''Most men look at me like they want me,'' the girl continued. ''Don't you feel that way?''

''It's not you,'' he said heavily. ''It's me—I'm on the run. There are two men on my trail now ''

Laurie stirred 'Why? I can't believe you'd run from anybody, or anything.''

''I'm dodging them because I don't want any more killing on my hands. I'm headed for Mexico.''

''Killing? You mean that you killed—shot somebody?''

''Yes. Was a time ago—''

''You're not the first to shoot down another man. I'm sure there was a good reason ''

''I figured there was,'' Temple said and broke off, seeing Morgan Cole rise glance about, and then hurry toward them. 'Here comes your brother.''

Laurie did not stir. Cole, his features stiff and angry in the sallow light, halted before them

''What's going on here?'' he demanded

''Nothing,'' the girl replied flatly. 'I was cold and couldn't sleep and came over here to talk to Temple.''

''You look pretty cozy under that poncho—''

''I was cold, and he shared it with me.''

Morgan continued to eye them suspiciously. Temple shook his head 'Back off, Cole All we've been doing is talk.''

Morgan gave that thought and nodded. ''I'll take your word for it—but I want to warn you! Don't let her talk you into something like she has Harley Edge. She'll do anything to get things her way. And you,'' he added, turning to Laurie 'Best you get back there where you belong—''

''And if I don't, what'll you do? Run home and tell Pa?'' Laurie demanded ıcily, getting to her feet.

Morgan's jaw hardened, and it looked again as if he would strike the girl, but Temple, drawing himself erect. brought about a change of mind

'Go on—get back to the others,'' he said and as ᴸaurıe moved past him finished 'And stay there.''

Both men were silent as they watched the girl move off, and then when she had settled down near Tom Gabriel, Cole turned to Temple.

"You want me to take over watching?" he asked brusquely.

"I'll call you when it's your turn," Temple replied coolly and resumed his place on the rock.

13

There was no letup in the force of the howling wind, and when daybreak came with the sun lurking behind a sky filled with a pale yellow cast, John Temple knew they were in for more trouble.

"Sand—sand and dust," he said with a shake of his head. "We're in for a bad sandstorm."

"I've seen sandstorms before," Morgan Cole said. "Ain't no reason why we can't go on."

"No, sure ain't. Certainly no point in staying here." It had become necessary to shout in order to be heard above the shrieking of the wind through the brush. "Good chance the storm will blow itself out in a few hours."

With that Temple turned to Ira Kelley, slumped against the tree to which he had handcuffed Philbin. The old lawman looked to be near collapse.

'What about you, Marshal? Figure you can go on?"

The lawman raised his drawn face, laid his deep-set, bloodshot eyes on his prisoner squatting on his heels close by.

"Sure—and I'll make it," he croaked. "Ain't nothing going to keep me from handing over Philbin to the law in Grant."

Clint laughed. "You ain't going to live long enough to do that, grandpa!"

"Maybe not," Kelley countered in a lagging voice that was almost lost in the wind, "but I sure aim to try. If something happens, howsomever," he added turning to Temple and the other men, "and I can't—I'm charging you fellows with doing it for me. It's your bounden duty as good, law-abiding citizens to see that this murdering snake gets what's coming to him."

"You'll make it all right, Marshal," Morgan Cole said. "Don't fret none about that."

"I ain't all that sure, boy. Maybe it was all them gooseberries and onions I ate, but things get kind of fuzzy, and I ain't got much starch in my knees. Now, if I peter out, you all go on—just take Philbin with you. Like I've done said, we've got to see that he gets what's coming to him."

"You're plumb loco!" the outlaw cut in. "Crazy as a mud coot—and flapping your jaws ain't—"

"We'll see that he's handed over to the sheriff in Grant," Tom Gabriel said, "but I expect you'll be doing that yourself."

"Maybe so, and I ain't about to give up—but if I don't make it I'll be obliged if all of you sees to it that my job's finished. We can't let no-good murdering trash like him run loose among decent folks again . . . I reckon I'm ready to start walking."

Gabriel stepped up to the lawman. "Sort of lean on me, Marshal, till you find your legs."

Temple, hanging the refilled canteen on his shoulder, glanced at the rancher. "Got any idea yet how far we are from that way station?"

Gabriel, now supporting Kelley, bobbed his head at Cole. "Can use a little help from you, friend," he said in a brittle tone, and then as Morgan crossed to Kelley's side, replied to Temple.

"Still can't be sure. My guess is that we ought to reach there by about the middle of the afternoon, but bucking this wind's going to slow us down plenty."

"Well, let's get started at it! Ain't going to get no easier," Clint Philbin said, brushing at his mouth. His small, sly eyes were on Laurie Cole as he spoke and were raking her appraisingly.

"Everybody got something to wear over your nose and mouth?" Temple asked, pulling his neck bandanna up to where it covered all of his face but his eyes. "Blowing sand's bad here where there's trees and brush, but it'll be ten times worse once we're out in the open."

His last words were probably lost to the masking bandanna and the wind, but he did not repeat them, simply waited and watched as the rest of the party followed his example after which all got underway— Temple in the lead with Laurie at his heels, after which came Philbin, Morgan Cole, who had alone assumed the assistance of Ira Kelley, and lastly Tom Gabriel, who, once again, seemed to be feeling the pain in his wounded arm more than before.

They made their way through the growth that clustered along the creek and then abruptly as they moved beyond its relative shelter stepped out into the full force of the storm.

Temple heard a faint cry from Laurie as the stinging sand lashed at her. Pausing, he reached out, caught her by the arm, and drew her in close.

"Keep in behind me," he shouted.

She nodded and immediately stepped in as near as possible, grateful for the protection his body afforded from the driving particles.

Temple, readjusting his bandanna, plodded on. It was not possible to look about to seek a better route. The sand and dust were like a wall around them, making it difficult to see more than ten feet or so in any direction. He was only certain they were moving toward the south—toward the way station at Doubtful Canyon—and that, only because he had fixed his course in mind back in the clearing along the creek.

It was not only the sand—sharp-edged bits of quartz, gypsum, granite, and other rock—that slowed their progress and made every step an effort, but the powerful wind lashing at them with unabated fury, buffeting them relentlessly, tearing at their clothing, and sapping their strength already diminished by the lack of food and rest, began to take its toll.

A faint shout reached Temple and brought him to a stop. Wheeling, he saw Gabriel and Cole exchanging positions, the cattleman now assuming the support of Ira Kelley.

"Let Philbin carry him!" he shouted.

But Gabriel, apparently not understanding, shook his head and motioned for the party to continue.

The minutes dragged painfully by and became an hour. There was no slackening of the storm, and it became clear that its dying off by midmorning—as was usual—seemed most unlikely. Temple began to have thoughts of the party being compelled to buck the hammering sand and wind for the entire day.

Some would be unable to withstand that, he knew; Ira Kelley for one—but Laurie Cole, it would be too much for her, or any woman. And there was Tom Gabriel to consider. Despite his stubborn determination to bear his share of the load regardless of an injured arm, he was in no condition to absorb such punishment indefinitely.

That left Morgan Cole, Philbin, and himself. Between them they perhaps could assist the others and eventually arrive at Doubtful Canyon—still an unknown distance ahead. Morgan, Temple supposed, would be willing to do his share for his own good, but the outlaw no doubt would be a problem.

Temple stumbled and almost went to his knees. Righting himself, he saw that the flat they had been crossing had broken off, and they were entering an arroyo, one fairly deep it appeared and somewhat below the general level of the surrounding land.

The force of the wind tapered off, and the sharp bite of the sand on his exposed skin was replaced by a thin, choking dust pall that hung overhead like a smothering canopy.

Continuing slowly on, almost feeling his way, Temple saw the raw, rough face of the arroyo wall a few steps to his right and angled toward it. A few minutes' rest out of the pitiless wind and sand would be a welcome relief. Reaching the embankment, he halted and, raising his hand, motioned for the stop and sat down. The howling was not so loud on the floor of the arroyo, and it would be less difficult to speak.

Uncorking the canteen Temple started it along the line of fellow travelers, backs huddled against the rugged wall—Laurie, Philbin, Morgan Cole, Marshal Kelley, and the rancher Tom Gabriel in that order. After each had taken a swallow and the container was again in his hands, Temple had his turn at relieving the dryness of his throat.

The cork again securely in place, Temple set the canteen on the ground and, rising, started for Ira Kelley. Immediately Philbin protested.

"Hell's fire—can't we stay here out of that damned wind for a bit? I ain't—"

Temple only shook his head and moved on. Reaching the lawman, he squatted and studied the man's pinched features closely. Kelley's brows and lashes were thick with dust, and his eyes were closed.

"He's in a bad way," Gabriel volunteered, "but I reckon he'll last as long as any of us. Man's got the guts of an army mule."

Temple smiled. "What I'd expect. Was thinking earlier we ought to make Philbin help with him some—and I'll do my share."

The cattleman shook his head. "Be better if you'll do just what you're doing—staying out front and keeping us going in the right direction. And forget Philbin. We can't trust him. Even if we took the marshal's gun so's he couldn't get his hands on it, he'd pull something tricky. Leave Kelley up to Cole and me—we'll see to him. . . . You think we might hole up here for awhile— maybe a half hour or so? Sure can use the rest."

Temple got to his feet. "Be a good idea. I'll scout on ahead a ways and see if this arroyo keeps going in the right direction. Can figure on me being back in fifteen minutes or less."

Laurie watched Temple move off into the haze of the arroyo, his tall, square-shouldered figure dim in the sifting dust. Upon impulse she started to rise and follow to continue their interrupted conversation but Clint Philbin's voice close to her ear halted her.

"We're wanting the same thing, little lady," he said. "We're both wanting loose—"

Laurie drew back slightly and stared at the outlaw. "What?"

"I've been listening to the things you and your brothe[r] keep chawing over—and last night, I heard what yo[u] and that Temple was saying—most of it. Sort of worke[d] my way up close to where you two was setting—clos[e] as I could with these damn cuffs chaining me to tha[t] tree. You was asking him to take you with him—beggin[g] him—"

"I didn't beg. I just thought—"

"You sure won't have to do no begging with me, n[o] ma'am! You just do what I tell you, and we'll both ge[t] what we're wanting."

Laurie considered Philbin's words absently. She wa[s] not the least interested in doing anything with him—a[n] outlaw of the very worst kind, she'd heard the men say.

"You and me, we could have us a high old time i[f] you wanted," she heard Clint continue. "I've got plenty of money stashed away—me and some friends have. I'd be right willing to take you with me, and then the two of us could go anywhere that suited you and live real fancy. You could be my woman, or if that'd bother you, we could go ahead and get ourselves married. I'd even do that for you, if that's the way you wanted it.

"And like I said, there wouldn't be no sweating about money. I've got plenty, and you could have everything you set your mind on. . . . All you've got to do is help me get shed of these here handcuffs—then you can leave the rest to me."

Being married to, or just living with, an outlaw, a killer, one with plenty of money—he claimed—who would take her away from all the unhappiness and dissatisfaction she faced with her pa, could be the answer. But could she stand to be the woman, or wife, of a man like Clint Philbin? He looked so dirty, so repulsive, and

96

evil—but still with a bath and a shave and some new clothes—

"Won't be no big chore, you getting the key to these cuffs. It's in the top pocket of the marshal's vest, left-hand side. You can sneak it easy—just go over there and sort of fuss around with him like women are always doing with some jasper when he's sort of laid up. When you get the key, slip it to me. Then when the time's just right, I'll make my move, and me and you'll be—"

Philbin broke off abruptly. John Temple's tall shape was looming in the pale haze ahead.

"What do you say, little lady? I can sure get you out of the fix you're in, and going with me—you'll sure have yourself a fine life."

Laurie watched Temple draw near, head pitched forward, face tipped down, eyes narrowed against the dust.

"I'll—I'll have to think about it," she murmured.

"What?" the outlaw pressed.

"I'll think about it," the girl repeated.

14

"Arroyo runs on like this for quite a ways," Temple said when he was again with Gabriel and the others. "Don't know just how far—could run on for miles. Cuts back toward the road."

"That good?" Morgan Cole wondered, getting to his feet.

"Better for it to veer that direction than angle off to some other. Sure don't want to lose our bearings."

"Might be smart to get back up on the road," Gabriel suggested. "Doubt if there'll be any Apaches hanging around waiting to jump pilgrims in this storm."

"You're probably right," Temple agreed. "We'll follow out the arroyo and see if it won't take us back to the road. If it don't, we'll swing off on our own."

The party began to assemble, Morgan Cole now taking over the assisting of Ira Kelley. The old lawman looked to be somewhat improved after the rest beyond the reach of the punishing wind. A change seemed to have come over Laurie, too, Temple noticed. It was if she had not only found new strength, but her fierce and stubborn independence was reasserting itself, and she was now less distraught and anxious.

He wondered, as they moved out, if she were regretting their conversation and was feeling embarrassment over having bared her heart and hopes to him. He wished now he had been more receptive and understanding and not turned her away so callously.

It would be wonderful to have Laurie for his wife. Earlier the thought had stirred him deeply, and he had briefly savored the idea but had quickly, for her sake, thrown up a wall of indifference to it. There was no place in his future for a wife. He'd be in Mexico, but just where and doing what was a question.

Like as not, he would be living in the open, a soldier constantly on the move, and that certainly would be no life for a girl like Laurie. She deserved, was entitled, to better, and he was not the kind of man who would subject her to less. He'd explain all that to her first chance he had.

It had been in his mind to do so that previous night while they were talking, but Morgan had appeared at that moment, and the opportunity passed. He'd get her aside, however, make her understand that, were it not for serious complications in the form of Amos Bell and Ford Kailer, matters between them could be different.

Temple glanced at the girl. She was a stride or so off to his right, her face, with the exception of her eyes, obscured by the blue scarf that she had been wearing over her head. In the dimness of the pall, she was a slender, well-shaped figure despite the condition of her clothing.

At that moment Clint Philbin, nearby, edged in closer and said something to the girl. Laurie shook her head, whereupon the outlaw dropped back and resumed his position.

Temple frowned. What had Kelley's prisoner said to the girl? It had been a question, there was no doubt of that; had he annoyed her in some way while they were sitting side by side during the rest the party had taken. Anger stirred through Temple. He'd ask Laurie about it and if Clint Philbin had bothered her, he'd straighten the man out mighty quick and let him know that he was to stay clear of the girl. It was too damn bad Marsha Kelley couldn't look after his prisoner instead of leaving it up to others.

Immediately John Temple shook that irritating thought from his mind. Ira Kelley didn't ask to get hurt. Had there not been the accident, he would be shepherding the outlaw just as he had been earlier. And the fact that the injury sustained incapacitated him should not be a source of personal resentment toward the lawman. A hard grin pulled at Temple's lips. He guessed it was the fact that Philbin had spoken with such familiarity to Laurie that irked him.

Kelley was walking on his own, he saw, as he let his gaze swing to the others. The wind was still howling, and its force had evidently decreased little if any at all. But they were all faring better out of its reach, and traveling was much easier in spite of the smothering dust that stung their eyes and made breathing difficult. They were fortunate to have stumbled onto the arroyo where the punishing blasts could reach them only infrequently.

Temple's stride broke. He lifted a hand in a signal to halt. Coming to him on the thick air was the distinct smell of smoke. They were some distance beyond the point he had reached earlier when scouting the deep wash, which would account for his not encountering the odor at that time.

"What is it?" Gabriel asked, moving up to Temple's side and then answered his own question. "Smoke! Apaches—that what you're figuring?"

"Could be," Temple replied, "and it could be a party of pilgrims—a wagon or two headed west."

Morgan Cole, joining them, said, "Ain't likely to be Indians. They wouldn't be making a fire—"

"Can't bank on that," Gabriel said, disagreeing. "On a day like this they probably figure there's nobody else around."

Laurie had turned to Temple and was watching him intently, her eyes dark and concerned above the covering on her face. Philbin had dropped to his haunches, while Ira Kelley, taking advantage of the stop, had found himself a seat on a weedy hummock.

"What do you think we ought to do?" Cole wondered. 'Be mighty risky to just go marching right up and—"

"Not what we'll do," Temple stated. "If it's a party of pilgrims, fine. We can get help—"

"What if it's a bunch of redskins?"

"That's about who it'll be. I can't figure how wagons could get down into this arroyo."

"Sure haven't seen no tracks—"

"Wind would have covered them over," Temple said, "but I don't think it'll be pilgrims. Most likely it's a party of Apaches hunkering down out of the wind—and that'll be fine."

"Fine?" Gabriel echoed.

"Yeh, Apaches'll mean horses, and if there ain't too many braves, we ought to be able to grab us enough mounts to ride to that way station."

Temple switched his attention to Laurie and Marshal Kelley. "Want you to sit tight right here—up close to the wall of the arroyo. If you hear shooting, hide in the brush till we show up."

"Best one of you fellows give me a hand with Philbin there," the lawman said, jerking a thumb at his prisoner.

"Don't want him trying something cute while you're gone."

Digging into a pocket in his vest, Kelley produced a key. "Unlock one of them cuffs, then snap it tight around a couple of them branches of that bush—real close to the ground. He won't be getting loose from that, and if he tries, I'll settle him down with a rap on the head."

Taking the key, Temple, with the aid of Morgan Cole, crossed to where the outlaw sat and cuffed him as directed to the base of a young mesquite, paying no attention to the steady cursing and grumbling that came from Philbin.

"With a bit of good luck we'll be back with horses," Temple said, coming back around and returning the key to the marshal.

"What if you don't come back a'tall?" Philbin demanded, twisting about in an effort to get more comfortable.

Temple glanced at Laurie and smiled reassuringly. "We'll be back," he said and with Cole and Gabriel at his side hurried off into the thick haze that filled the arroyo.

15

With Temple in the lead they moved down the arroyo at a fast walk. There was no need to maintain silence as the moaning of the wind sweeping across the flat above the deep cut covered all other sounds. But it would be necessary to employ some degree of caution; in the blinding, filtering dust that filled the wash, they could come upon the encamped party unexpectedly and betray their presence.

Such would pose no problem if they proved to be pilgrims sheltering in the arroyo to escape the terrible blow, but if they were Apaches, as he expected them to be, he and the two men with him were in for trouble, as the braves generally traveled in parties of a half dozen or more.

The odor of smoke was stronger. Temple once again raised his hand to signal a halt. "Not far ahead," he warned.

"Being downwind ought to let us work in real close," Gabriel said.

Temple nodded and drawing his pistol motioned for Cole and Gabriel to do likewise, then, hunched low, he resumed the approach toward the unseen camp. A hundred feet later he again paused. Suddenly he dropped to the floor of the wash. Gabriel and Morgan Cole followed his move instantly.

Directly ahead a fire flickered erratically in the vagrant puffs of wind dipping down into the arroyo. Seven Apaches sat about it in a circle, some dozing, others eating bits of meat that had apparently been roasted over the flames.

"That the same bunch that jumped the stage?" Morgan asked in a tense whisper.

"Could be—but I doubt it—"

"Damn! That rabbit sure smells good," Gabriel murmured. "You spot the horses?"

"Tied up in that brush off to the left there behind them," Temple replied.

"Yeh—I see them now—in the dark shadows," the cattleman said. "We can't get to them over there without going through those redskins."

"They're not expecting anything," Temple said. "Good chance we can circle around to the horses, and the braves won't ever see us."

Morgan Cole swore softly. "Hell, why don't we just start shooting? Time they figured out what hit them, they'd all be dead."

"No need doing any more killing than we just have to," Temple replied. "Anyway, shots could draw another bunch that's maybe somewhere close."

"We ain't sure there are more—"

"No, but we can't be sure there's not either, and we sure better not gamble on it," Temple said and turned to Gabriel. "How do you feel about it, Tom?"

The cattleman brushed at his eyes. "Shooting would be too risky—like you said. Let's try circling. Most of those braves are sleeping, and if we're lucky, we can get us something to ride without a fight."

Temple said no more and, dropping back a short distance, led the way up and out of the arroyo onto the flat above. The wind greeted them with a howling blast that ripped and tore at them mercilessly while sand particles peppered and stung their exposed skin. Heads lowered and bodies leaning forward, they swung wide of the area where the Indians were camped and when well below, returned to the deep wash.

The relief at being out of the frightful blow was instantaneous and welcome, and for a time they remained motionless, leaning slackly against the wall of the wash, lungs heaving, eyes burning, and mouths gritty while they recovered breath and strength. Only when each had fully recovered did they continue, approaching the Apache renegades from below now instead of above.

They had swung well to the south of the camp, Temple saw. Keeping close to the side of the arroyo and the ragged growth—rabbit brush, plume, Mormon tea, and mesquite—they worked their way toward the fire, little more than a pale orange circle in the thick dust.

A few yards short of their goal Temple stopped and drew in behind a clump of the brush. The braves were now visible, hunched, vague figures in the murk-restricted flare of light. One stirred, sat for several moments staring into the flames, and then picking up a handful of sticks lying nearby tossed them into the fire. As the flames brightened and a hurried crackling arose, two of the other braves shifted restlessly but settled back down.

When all appeared quiet, Temple resumed the cautious approach to the horses. Closing in on the animals, regardless of how much care was employed, would be a difficult job, he knew. It was necessary to come at the ponies from their lower side. What wind there was reaching down into the arroyo would carry their scent to the horses. They would shy, disturbed by the smell of white men, and could set up a racket that would arouse the dozing braves.

But there was nothing to be done about it; they would simply have to move slow and easy until they reached the horses, free them—fortunately they were tethered by ropes to the brush, not hobbled as was often the way of Indians—then lead the animals back through the wash.

In the pale yellowish gloom Temple motioned to Morgan Cole, indicating that he was to take the first two horses when they were close enough and move off quietly with them along the route the three of them had just come. Cole nodded his understanding.

He gave the same instructions to Gabriel with the exception that the rancher was to take charge of the next two ponies in the line. He, coming last, would handle the next pair which would enable him to bring up the rear as they headed back down the arroyo. He preferred that position since he was unsure of both Morgan Cole and Gabriel should trouble develop and gunplay become necessary.

They moved on silent as smoke as they worked their way along the brush, taking advantage of the shadows and an occasional canopy of overhanging brush. When within only a stride of the first pony, which was showing signs of nervousness, Temple beckoned Cole forward and allowed him to pass by and ease up to the first of the ponies.

At that moment one of the renegades stirred. Temple murmured a warning. Cole and Gabriel froze, as did he. The brave stretched and got to his feet. Bending over, he gathered up some of the dry wood from the pile near him and, like the brave before him, threw it onto the fire. But there the similarity stopped. Instead of resuming

106

his place in the circle, he came about and started toward the horses.

The Apache halted abruptly. In the dusty pall aglow now with light from the fire's surging flames, Temple saw the renegade's head come back in surprise, heard the startled yell that exploded from his lips, and watched him bend swiftly and snatch up the rifle lying at his feet and whirl.

Temple fired from the hip as the remainder of the renegade party, aroused by the brave's shout, leaped to their feet. At once they began to trigger their weapons and loose arrows. By that moment Gabriel and Cole had their guns out and were making use of them.

Three of the braves, including the one who had sounded the alarm, were down. Temple heard Morgan Cole curse, glanced around, and saw that he had taken an arrow in the thigh. But the braves were backing off, breaking away from the fire and its silhouetting light, and seeking refuge in the dark beyond.

"By God—we've done it!" Temple heard Gabriel say in a breathless sort of voice when a fourth renegade dropped. "We've got ourselves some horses, and—"

A chorus of wild yells coming from the wash below them cut short the cattleman's words of triumph. Temple spun. Through the dust haze he could see a dozen or more figures rushing toward them. Temple swore angrily. Apaches! Another party of renegades. They had heard the gunshots and were hurrying to aid their kin.

"This way!" he shouted to Cole and Gabriel and, crowding past the now frantic Indian ponies thrashing about in an effort to free themselves of their tie ropes, climbed the wall of the arroyo up onto the windswept flat above.

Waiting only long enough to be certain Tom Gabriel

and Cole were behind him, Temple ran straight ahead into the teeth of the gusting blow.

"Wrong way!" he heard Morgan Cole shout.

Temple only shook his head and continued. It would be a fatal error to strike for the upper end of the wash where Laurie, Marshal Kelley, and his prisoner were waiting. The Apaches would be in close pursuit, and such made it imperative they lead the renegade braves away from, not to, the others in the party.

Fighting the fierce, driving wind with its stinging sand for a good two hundred yards, Temple finally slowed and when Gabriel and Cole were alongside, halted. Drawing his pistol, he aimed it in the direction he knew the Apaches would most likely be and fired two quick shots as if to repel the renegades.

Gabriel and Cole, backs placed to the wind, stared at him wonderingly. The latter said; "Hell, that won't do no good! We can't even see them."

"But they'll see that powder flash and keep coming this way," Temple explained, reloading his weapon. "We've got to pull them away from the arroyo."

Moving on, Temple began to curve left. Shortly they came to a second wash, one considerably smaller in both width and depth than the first in which they had earlier taken refuge. Dropping into it, he led his companions, all breathing heavily from running, along its meandering, southerly course for a short distance and then, abandoning it, once again veered left.

Minutes later they came to the main arroyo and, crossing it, began to circle northward. With the hammering wind now at their backs it was easier to travel faster, and when they had covered what Temple figured to be the necessary distance, they once more cut left. He could only guess at the exact location of the arroyo and whether they were above or below Laurie Cole and the others. Since all landmarks had been hidden in the swirling sand and dust when they first came to the big arroyo, he had nothing to judge location by now; he could only rely on instinct.

Minutes later they reached the deep wash and leaped down into it. Pausing to recover his breath, Temple considered the restricted area in which they found themselves, hopeful of recognizing a familiar object or formation in the wall of the arroyo.

From nearby Cole said, "You figure we shook them Apaches?"

"If things went right, they're somewheres west and south of us, so I reckon we're all right for a while," Temple replied "But we best find the others and get out of here fast. . . . I'm trying to figure out whether they're above or below us."

Gabriel, still sucking hard for breath, wiped at his mouth. "Below us, I'd say."

"My guess too," Temple said and, delying no further, struck off down the wash at a fast walk.

They were right. A quarter mile later they reached Laurie and the two men, all pulled back in the brush hiding, as they had been warned to do.

"Heard shots," Ira Kelley said as he came stiffly to his feet. "Been so long we was beginning to think you'd got into real trouble."

Temple helped himself to the key in the lawman's vest pocket, released Philbin from the mesquite, then joined the outlaw's wrists together once more.

"Got jumped by another bunch of Indians," he heard Gabriel explain. "Just about had us some horses when one of them woke up—they were all setting around a fire sleeping—and hollered. That was the shooting you heard."

"We was doing all right too," Morgan Cole added, stuffing a handkerchief obtained from his sister into the arrow wound in his leg. Although it was shallow, it had bled copiously. "We would have had them horses if that other bunch hadn't showed up."

"So what're we going to do now?" Kelley wanted to know, taking the handcuff key from Temple and restoring it to its place in his pocket. "Sure won't be healthy around here."

"We'll have to move on," Temple said simply, reaching for Laurie's hand to assist her as he started to climb the embankment. "Means we're going to be bucking that wind again, but we've got no choice."

16

Once out of the arroyo John Temple struck a northerly course, one that would take him and the others away from the deep wash, which the Apaches were certain to search eventually, and in the direction of the road.

They pushed on woodenly, buffeted by the maddening, ceaseless wind and whipped by the stinging blasts of sand. Ira Kelley began to weaken again under the lash of the storm, and within the hour Temple began to watch for a hollow, a cluster of trees—anyplace where they could take refuge for a short rest.

They paused a time later in the lee of a fairly large rocky butte upon the crown of which chaparral, snake-weed, and other scrub growth was whipping wildly about. It was a stop of short duration. Temple felt they were still not far enough removed from the area where the Apaches would be searching to be safe.

Thus a quarter hour later they were again on the move, trudging wearily along, bucking a wind that had lost none of its force. It was growing late in the day, Temple realized, and they would again be faced with spending a night in the open with no food and little water. The thought sent a wave of frustration rushing through him. *Where the hell was the damned way station? Could they have bypassed it?*

In the dense murk of dust and sand while the wind was hammering at them constantly with their heads down and eyes all but shut tight, he reckoned they could have missed the settlement—possibly by as little as fifty yards. The likelihood set up a worry in Temple's mind, and at the next halt an hour or so later, he mentioned the probability to Gabriel and Cole.

The rancher, squatting on his heels behind a clump of rabbit brush, wiped at his red-rimmed eyes with a bandanna.

"Sure a good chance of it, can't deny that," he admitted, "but I don't think so."

Morgan was not so certain. "The place ain't much— you can't call Doubtful Canyon a real town. Got a saloon, a general store, maybe a half a dozen houses besides the way station with its barns and corral. In this blasted windstorm where a man can't see no more'n twenty or thirty feet, we could have gone right on by."

"Seems we ought've come to the road somewhere before that," Gabriel said.

"And what about a crossroad—the one that goes east to west?" Temple wondered. 'We would have come to it, wouldn't we?"

"Maybe," the rancher said, "but it sort of goes south before it swings east for the next town—Franklin— near as I recollect."

Laurie, sitting on a rock nearby, hands folded in her lap, sighed deeply. Hunger and fatigue sagged her young body, sharpened the lines in her face, and dulled her eyes, but she had uttered no word of complaint. Laurie Cole was one hell of a lot of woman, Temple decided, studying her covertly—one any man would be proud to call his wife and make any sacrifice for.

"I just don't figure we've come far enough," Gabriel

said after a few moments consideration. 'The way station is still up ahead—somewheres.''

"We been walking damn near a whole day," Clint Philbin declared sourly. "I'm beginning to think you jaspers have got us lost. . . . And something else, I'm still hungry, mighty hungry! I want something to eat."

"What the hell you think the rest of us are doing—filling up on this here sand and dust?" Ira Kelley demanded. "We're all hungry, so you just shut up and let these fellows do the best they can. You ain't going to starve—you're too damn mean!"

"Sure feels like I'm about to starve," the outlaw grumbled and turned his attention to Laurie. "I can see you're feeling the same way, missy—ain't that right? Sure would be nice to be setting in a fine restaurant in New Orleans, or maybe some other big town, all dressed up in fancy duds and having a supper of—"

"Forget it, Clint," Temple cut in. "Talk like that only makes things harder—"

"Ain't meaning to do that," Philbin said with a sly wink at Laurie. "Was only saying how nice it could be, was things different—sort of reminding her."

"I don't need to be reminded of anything," the girl replied and looked away.

"I vote we just keep going the way we are," Tom Gabriel said. "We're bound to hit a road sooner or later, either the one from Cottonwood or the one that goes to Franklin. Way I see it, we just plain can't be far from something."

"That's how I look at it," Temple agreed, "but in all this dust and sand, a man's got nothing to go on but his sense of direction—and I've got to the point where I'm sort of doubting mine."

"Far as I'm concerned you're pointing right," Ira

Kelley said. "I've got a feel for directions too, and I've got a hunch we're about to come to the Cottonwood road."

Kelley was right. A long, exhausting two hours later with the already dim world that enclosed them growing even darker as the day began to end, they came suddenly onto the roadway's rutted surface.

Relief and satisfaction flowed through Temple as he led the party up onto it. Doubtful Canyon now had to be somewhere ahead, that was a certainty—but just how far was the question, and night was upon them.

"Best thing we can do is cross over," Temple said, still wary of the renegade Indians, "and follow the road till we come to a place where we can spend the night. By morning the storm ought've blown itself out, and maybe we can then get an idea of where we are."

The others agreed. "Going to have to find something to eat," Temple continued. "Expect there'll be some rabbits in the brush. Tom, you and Morgan move off to the sides and see if you can't scare us up a couple. I'll keep my eyes peeled in the front."

"How'll we get them?" Cole asked. "Don't dare shoot. We ain't sure where them Indians are."

"Don't use your gun, for sure," Temple replied. "Take a club instead. In this kind of a storm the rabbits will be as bad off as we are, hardly seeing or hearing anything, and you'll find them setting around under the bushes."

"You think building a fire to roast them'll be smart?"

"It'll be risky, but I've got an idea how to handle it," Temple said. "You catch us a couple of rabbits, and I'll do the rest."

Laurie Cole, chewing on a tough but welcome bit of thoroughly cooked jackrabbit, looked across the shel-

114

tered clearing at Temple. He had done just as he had promised and without endangering them insofar as the Apaches were concerned. The place he had found for the night camp was at the foot of a bluff which rose between the small bit of open ground and the aggravating nerve-wracking wind and was effectively screened from view on its opposite side by a dense stand of brush.

Not long after they had stopped, and she had sunk gratefully onto a clump of grass near exhaustion, Morgan and the rancher Gabriel appeared with not two but three rabbits they had managed to kill. After skinning and dressing them out, Temple had moved away from the camp at what was apparently a considerable distance downwind and there built a fire over which he roasted the small animals. He did so, Gabriel had explained to her, so that if the smell of smoke drew the Apaches, it would not lead them to the camp.

Temple was the man for her, Laurie decided in a sudden burst of conviction. He was everything any woman could want—strong, capable, with the ability to meet and overcome any problem regardless of how serious, yet gentle and considerate.

But so far he had shown no great interest in her, at least not enough to take her for his wife—or woman. Thus she had to face up to making a choice between her two other possibilities—Harley Edge, who would be waiting at Doubtful Canyon when they arrived which would probably be, according to what she had overheard, sometime that following morning; or Clint Philbin, the outlaw.

Of course there was Tom Gabriel. She had not thought of him earlier, but now that avenue of escape entered her mind. She discarded the idea almost as quickly as it had come; Gabriel was a rancher with a spread somewhere to the north of her pa's. If she defied her parent and married Gabriel, she could expect her pa to sooner or later send a dozen or so Circle C hired hands over to burn down the Gabriel place, poison the water holes, or fire the range grass in the hope that by bankrupting Tom Gabriel he could force her back home. No, Gabriel, even if she could interest him, was out of the question.

That left Harley Edge or the outlaw. That realization brought to mind the jingle that had been current among the girls at the schoolhouse in Pastor Valley when the subject of marriage came up: *Would you rather be a young man's slave or an old man's plaything?*

Harley Edge—he would be the young man, one with little future other than being a fence-riding cowhand doomed to a life of poorly paid labor. She could substitute the word *outlaw* for *old man* and thus would have Clint Philbin, making the bit of doggerel fit her predicament.

Harley or Clint Philbin—which was it to be? One thing certain, she must decide soon for once they reached Doubtful Canyon she must have her mind made up.

Why couldn't it be Temple? Why couldn't she have been fortunate enough to attract him? The self-imposed question brought a sense of frustration to her. She was considered attractive and intelligent; why didn't she appeal to him?

It had something to do with his past, Laurie suddenly remembered, recalling their conversation that first night when she had shamelessly bared her heart to him. He had said he'd killed somebody, that two men were following him, and that he was endeavoring to escape to Mexico. It was hard to imagine Temple as a cold-blooded killer, but she reckoned he could be if he so desired. He was all strength and resolution—that was plain—and if

116

he were forced to do something such as kill another man, he undoubtedly would do so without hesitation.

He had started to explain matters to her when Morgan had awakened and come looking for her. Hope began to stir through Laurie. Maybe that was the key; maybe if she knew why he was on the run, she could reason with him and not only change his mind about Mexico but about her as well.

She had a feeling that Temple actually was drawn to her. Twice she had caught him looking closely at her in the way that other men, wanting her, had done. Now that she thought about it, it was as if he were afraid to let her become a part of his life! Well, she'd see about that!

But she'd best let things ride until morning. Temple, after setting up a watch schedule with Morgan and Gabriel, had stretched out along the base of the bluff and was already asleep Besides, she wanted to think things through.

17

Near dawn that next morning the storm blew itself out, and an eerie sort of calm settled over the land. Temple, who had stood the final leg of the night's guard duty, roused the others, and they prepared to resume the journey to Doubtful Canyon

"Thank God that damn sand's quit blowing!" Tom Gabriel said fervently. "Walking won't be so bad now."

Temple agreed 'Only thing," he pointed out, "we'll have to keep to the low ground as much as possible. The Apaches'll find it easy to spot us when we're in the open "

Morgan Cole overheard the comment. Staring off to the south, the direction in which they would be traveling, he wiped at his dust-streaked face as he shook his head.

'Staying out of sight ain't going to be easy. Hardly anything but flats ahead of us."

Temple pointed to a line of low hills off to their left. 'It'll be smart, I figure to take the time to work over to them. Be out of our way a bit, I'll admit, but there looks to be a lot brush growing along the foot of them "

"And just maybe there'll be another deep arroyo we can climb down into." Gabriel said and turned to Ira Kelley. The lawman was on his feet, but his features were wan and pinched and his eyes were bright with

118

pain. "You going to be all right, Marshal? It can't be too far now."

"Reckon I am," Kelley replied. "Just move out when you're ready. I'll be coming."

"The old man's damn near dead if you ask me," Philbin said. "Was you smart, you'd leave him right here and quit bothering with him."

"You sure would like that now, wouldn't you?" the marshal snapped, temper strengthening his voice. "When we get to that there settlement, I'll be right with you, killer, with my iron pointing straight at your guts, so don't go doing no hopeful wishing!"

Temple moved off, not troubling to listen to the outlaw's rejoinder. Kelley, through sheer will and regardless of pain, would no doubt do just as he declared.

Laurie Cole, Temple saw, was off to one side, her arms folded and held close to her body in an effort to ward off the early morning chill. Removing his poncho, he draped it about her shoulders. Startled, she came about.

"I—I didn't hear you—"

He smiled. "Not hard to believe that. You were doing some mighty deep thinking."

Laurie nodded. "Yes, I suppose I was," she replied and started to remove the poncho to return it to him. "I really don't need this, and you—"

"Better keep it," Temple said. "Cold doesn't bother me much—and that jacket of yours ain't much better than nothing at all. You can hand it back when it gets warmer."

Laurie made no further protest, and, features wiped clean with a moistened handkerchief, eyes partly closed, she stared off into the distance. "Would it surprise you,

119

Temple, to know that I was thinking about you back there a bit ago when you came up?''

''Yes, I reckon it would,'' he admitted and then shrugged. ''Pretty sure there's plenty of better things for you to be mulling about in your head.''

The girl made no reply to that but continued to look out over the flats. Then, ''Do you think we are near the way station now?''

Temple turned his glance to the south. ''Can't be too far, that's for certain. We've come a far piece since the Apaches wrecked that stage—and that was the halfway point.''

Abruptly Laurie faced him. ''Temple, can I walk with you awhile—just the two of us, I mean? There's something I want to ask—''

He studied her solemnly for several moments and then nodded. ''Sure—''

The girl wanted to talk about her problem, he guessed. They would reach Doubtful Canyon sometime that day, likely before noon, and she would need to make her decision either to do as her pa wished or to slip away from her brother, meet with Harley Edge, the cowhand he'd heard mentioned, and go with him.

Temple felt a twinge of regret as the party moved out of the clearing at the foot of the bluff and headed for the hills to the east. He wished he could be the man that Laurie chose; she was a most desirable woman and had shown an interest in him. But he had cooled all such feelings on the girl's part quickly, impressing upon her that his future was too uncertain and that there was no place in it for her.

That brought to mind the fact that somewhere behind them were the two men he was endeavoring to elude—Ford, the brother of Ned and Bill Kailer, and the

Pinkerton detective, Amos Bell, whom their father had hired to track him down.

They could be on the road at that moment, having waited somewhere until the storm had passed, or they could have pushed on regardless and now be at Doubtful Canyon waiting for him to put in an appearance. He had best assume that it would be the latter, take the necessary precautions, and continue to avoid any confrontation. Of course, as he had thought before, the two men could have fallen victims to the Apaches, and if so, he had no reason to fear them. Not that old Benjamin Kailer would let it drop! He'd see to it that another detective was—

"Temple—"

Laurie's voice at his shoulder brought him back to the moment. They had reached the first outcropping of brush that flowed out irregularly from the short hills. Tom Gabriel in the foremost of the straggling party was followed by Philbin, Ira Kelley, and Morgan Cole, who was lending what support he could to the lawman.

"Yeh?"

"Will you tell me something?"

Temple, bringing up the rear of the lagging group with the girl at his side, nodded. "Reckon so, if I can."

"You can. The truth is, you started to tell me once before—what it is you're running from—the other night, but Morgan came up, and you didn't finish."

"I remember," he said, reluctant as always to narrate the bitter time in his life to an outsider. But perhaps she was entitled to an explanation that would give her a better understanding of his position and why things had to be as they were.

"Goes back to the war," he said. "Don't think folks out in this part of the country got into it much."

"No, they didn't. We only got bits and pieces of news at the ranch. It seemed very far away."

"Then you would've never heard of what happened in Missouri where I—my family—lived."

"That where you're from?"

"Yes, Missouri. Folks had a farm in Bates County—three hundred and twenty acres laying along the Kansas line. Was my pa and ma and two sisters. They were twelve and fourteen when I enlisted in the Union Army and went off to fight."

"Most people around here were for the South—"

"I know. Every man has his own idea of what's right and what's wrong, I guess. I thought the Union ought to be preserved—that's why I joined with Lincoln's forces—but there were a lot of Missourians who believed in the South and its cause.

"I signed up late in sixty-one and done my bit right up to the battle at a place called Spottsylvania Court House. Got captured there and spent the rest of the war in a Reb prison."

"That must have been terrible—"

Temple's eyes, filled with a sort of lifeless emptiness, were reaching out across the flats and the hills to the higher Peloncillo Mountains on to the west.

"Was, but I've about got the recollection of it out of my mind now—leastwise, I don't think of it often any more. Anyway, when they turned us loose at the end of the war, I headed for home. I hadn't heard from them for years—the mail being what it was—and I was anxious to see the family, but when I got there I found there was nothing left. Everything had been burned to the ground, and my family, my parents and two sisters, were gone.

"I hunted up some neighbors that lived in the next county, and they told me what had happened. My family was dead—all of them. It was on account of an order issued by a Union general named Ewing—Order Number Eleven, it was called.

"There had been some guerrilla raids into Kansas—a man named Quantrill was the one they blamed—and this Ewing claimed that folks living along the border hid Quantrill and his bunch of outlaws—that's all they were—from the soldiers after there'd been a raid. He sort of overlooked the fact that Quantrill and his bunch were Confederates, while most of the Missouri people in the area were loyal to the Union.

"Seems Ewing was determined to stop Quantrill and others like him, so he put out this order to all the folks living along the Kansas border to move and gave them only a couple of weeks to do so. They were to just pick up and leave—no exceptions unless they could furnish proof that they were loyal to the Union, and there were hardly any who could come up with the kind of proof Ewing wanted."

"He was a Union general, and you were a soldier in the Union Army, and yet he—"

"I reckon my folks pointed that out to him, but it evidently didn't do any good. They had to load up what they could and move, but before they and some of the other folks living along the border could get out of the area, a lot of Ewing's solders and Union guerrillas rode in on them, robbed them of everything that had any value, burned what was left—and carried off the young women and girls.

"My pa died trying to protect my sisters. Same happened to my ma. Four men—soldiers—took the girls to a shack that we'd used to store feed. When they were through with them, both were dead."

"Oh, dear God!" Laurie murmured in a shocked voice.

"They weren't the only ones to end up in the hand of guerrillas and trash soldiers, but they were my kin and when I found out from some folks who'd been neighbors who the four men were that had wiped out my family and home, I started tracking them down.

"All four were Missourians—from the county seat east of us. Turned out two of them—men I didn't know—got killed towards the end of the war, but the other two, Bill and Ned Kailer, were still around. Their pa had a big farm besides being in a couple of businesses. Was a rich man and had a lot of pull with the politicians and the army.

"It didn't matter to me who they were. I looked up the Kailers, told them who I was and that I knew what they'd done—and that I'd come to kill them. I did, shot them both dead."

Laurie nodded understandingly. Up ahead Clint Philbin was railing at Marshal Ira Kelley, who was supporting himself by resting a hand on Morgan Cole's shoulder. Hearing the outlaw, Gabriel slowed, looked back, and then continued.

"What happened after that?" Laurie asked.

"Kailer, like I said, was a big man around there. I got caught and thrown in jail before I could turn myself into the sheriff. Laid around behind bars for quite a time, and then there was a trial, and although there were some folks who testified to what had happened to my family, I was convicted and sentenced to hang. Old Benjamin Kailer was just too big and powerful for people to buck.

"All but one. The deputy that was assigned to take me to the pen knew me and the family and what the

Kailer boys had done to them. He made it easy for me to escape. I did—headed into Kansas and then on north to the Dakota Territories and finally wound up in Wyoming. Did a bit of fur trapping but spent most of my time working on cattle ranches.

"Things went along fine. The war, and what had happened back in Missouri was sort of behind me, and then one day—I'd been up there about two years, I guess—I got word that a detective was snooping around looking for me. He'd been hired by Kailer to track me down, and Kailer had sent along his other son Ford to see that the job was done right."

"They the men who are following you now?"

Temple nodded. "The same . . . I didn't want any more killings on my hands—sure had nothing against the detective old Ben Kailer had hired, and Ford Kailer wasn't in on what was done to my family—so I quit my job, sold my horse and gear, and caught the stage going south.

"Doing that I gave the detective and Kailer the slip. They didn't figure on me heading south, I guess, thought I'd duck over into Canada to the north. But it didn't take them long to get back on my trail. The detective, he's a Pinkerton agent I learned, is a smart one. Found me working on a ranch in Colorado, so I took off south again—this time for Mexico. Friend of mine said he'd get me lined up with Benito Juarez and his army—"

"Indians! Apaches!" Gabriel sang out suddenly.

18

Temple halted in midstep, one hand catching Laurie Cole's arm and stopping her also. A half mile farther on a dozen braves had ridden out of a spur of trees, paused, and were looking toward the road, a short distance to the west of them.

"Into the brush—quick!" Temple snapped, pivoting

The others wheeled and as one rushed into the tangled growth a few strides to their left. Well within the stand of mesquite and like rank shrubs, Morgan Cole spoke up.

"You figure they spotted us?"

"Can't be sure, but I don't think so. Had their eyes on the road—looking for pilgrims, I expect," Temple replied and, removing his hat, moved to the outer edge of the brush and peered around it. Abruptly he returned.

"They're coming this way," he said in a low, tight voice. "I want everybody down—low—behind a rock or a thick bush—and no talking."

Immediately the party reacted, doing exactly as directed. Temple, after making certain that all were concealed, was the last to find a hiding place—a clump of reddish desert broom that thrust itself upward from beneath a fairly large rock.

Motionless, scarcely breathing, they awaited the

Apaches. The sun was well up by then, and its heat was making itself felt. Laurie, still wearing the wool poncho Temple had given her earlier, was noticing it most of all and no doubt wished she could rid herself of the garment but made no move to do so.

The moments ticked into minutes which, in turn, dragged by with exaggerated slowness. Insects resumed their noisy clacking in the grass and weeds, and a pair of doves, wings whistling, fluttered into a nearby paloverde, settled on one of the tree's higher branches, and glanced nervously about.

The first Indian suddenly appeared—a young buck, naked except for a breech cloth and a ragged band around his head. He sat hunched forward on his pony, rifle clutched in one hand, sun glistening on his sweaty copper-colored body. As was the custom of Indians, who believed saddles hindered their horses, the brave was riding bareback, his feet in ankle-high cowhide moccasins dangling limply at the sides of his mount.

The second Indian was little different; a bit older, perhaps, and like the first and those who followed—a dozen or so—had his dark eyes fixed on the not too distant road.

When they had passed and were well beyond earshot, Gabriel came to his feet. "They're sure looking for somebody! Can bet on it."

Temple agreed. "Could be us," he said, moving to where he could see the Apaches now disappearing beyond a hill.

The rancher pulled off his hat and ran his fingers through his damp hair. "Could be at that. Bunch tallies up to about the same number as them in the arroyo—after the others showed up."

The braves were out of sight. Temple came back

around and faced the party. Ira Kelley was still sittin
on the rock where he had settled when the warnin
came to hide, his features pinched and drawn from pai
and weariness. Crouched next to Laurie Cole, Philbi
was watching the girl intently as she divested herself c
the poncho. After a few moments he spoke softly t
her.

"We're running out of time, missy—"

Laurie hesitated, considered the outlaw for a lon;
breath, and then shifted her attention to Temple. Tossin;
him the poncho, she said, "Thank you for letting m
use this."

Temple, wondering at the meaning of the outlaw':
words, accepted the garment without comment. Laurie
saw the question in his eyes, but she made no offer tc
explain, and he shrugged off the incident and turned
again toward the Apaches, wanting to make certain they
had not reappeared. There was no sign of them.

"Can move on now," he said, resuming his place in
the lead of the party, "but stay close to the brush."

The others signified their understanding, and with the
morning's heat rising steadily and all traces of the wind
and sandstorm of the previous day and night gone, they
continued on their way.

Immediately Temple noticed that Laurie Cole was no
longer nearby, that she was now walking alone and
occupied in deep thoughts—thoughts, perhaps, of what
lay ahead for her at Doubtful Canyon and of the decision
that she would have to make.

He wondered how she now felt toward him after
being told of the things that shadowed his past. Undoubtedly she understood why he had nothing to offer any
woman—particularly her—in the way of a future. Life
with him in Mexico, one where she would be subjected

128

to the most primitive conditions and dragged about in the barren, rugged hills from camp to camp—such certainly was not for Laurie Cole.

Temple wished he could be of more help to her. She had become important to him—more important than he would let her know—and it troubled him to think of her being so unhappy. Too, that was not likely to change once they reached the way station, and she was forced to make her decision.

Was Clint Philbin now, in some way, involved? The glances she and the outlaw had exchanged and the guarded words that had passed between them seemed to indicate such. But it could hardly be possible. Philbin was an outlaw and even if he were free, and not on his way to prison, Laurie surely wouldn't take up with him. Or would she?

Was the girl desperate enough to fall in with some plan the outlaw had devised to escape from Ira Kelley with her help after which Clint would take Laurie with him as a reward for assisting him? It was a wild, improbable thought, and Temple was certain it was not possible; but down deep within him he knew that Laurie, in defiance of her father and determined to have her way, would stop at nothing.

Tom Gabriel would have to make up his mind, too, when they reached the way station, which surely was only a few miles distant now. It would be up to him to decide if he truly wanted the saloon woman, Cinnamon, for his wife, or if he intended to let neighbors and relatives determine his future.

Tom would never be happy if he chose the latter course, and he should bear in mind that it was he who would be making a life with the woman he chose, not one of his friends or relatives. It was his happiness and

129

contentment that counted—the rancher should not lose sight of that.

The day, hot and breathless, wore on. At noon they halted in the shade of a mesquite and ate the last of the rabbit each had stowed away in a pocket for such. The canteen, now running low again, was passed around and all had a swallow of its tepid contents.

"Hell, we can't be far from that damned way station now!" Morgan Cole declared almost angrily. "We've walked far enough to be in Arizona by now, seems."

"For sure!" Philbin grumbled. "I'm mighty tired of—"

"You've got a long rest coming to you, killer," Ira Kelley said in an exhausted voice, "so don't go bellyaching about being tired. Where you're going, resting's about all you'll have to do."

"Don't bamboozle yourself, old man! This here song's still got one more verse!"

"Well, you ain't going to sing it," the lawman said as they continued wearily on.

Temple again glanced at Laurie, still quiet and having no words for anyone. Once he watched Morgan angle over to her and say something in a low voice. The girl merely shrugged and stared straight ahead. Temple wished he might reach out to her to comfort her in some way, but she seemed to prefer only her own company, and he thought it best to respect her wishes.

"There's the way station!"

It was Tom Gabriel who again shouted the words, this time welcome ones.

"Over there—close to them little hills. Can see the tin roof of the saloon shining in the sun."

19

Laurie breathed a sigh of relief. Kelley swore, expressing his satisfaction at arriving, finally, at the settlement, or at least having it in sight. Morgan Cole had no comment, but the gratification was evident on his sun and wind scoured features just as it was on those of Temple and the rancher, Tom Gabriel. Philbin, on the other hand, appeared to be irritated as he stared off across the flats, now shimmering with heat. Kelley took note of the outlaw's attitude.

"What's chawing you, killer? You real put out because them friends of yours ain't showed up?"

"Who said they was?" Philbin demanded and then added coyly, "We ain't got there yet, grandpa."

"Same as," Kelley replied. "Two maybe three hours from right now, and you'll be roosting behind bars in Grant—and I'll be shut of you. That sure will be a good feeling."

Philbin said no more, and the party moved on, angling now toward a spur of trees and brush thrusting out of the higher hills to their left, about midway to the settlement.

Temple swung his eyes to Laurie and wondered what her thoughts might be as she drew near the point where her future was to be decided. Again he felt something stir within him, and once more he wished that matter between them could be different—that he could forsake his life of being forever on the run, take Laurie Cole for his wife, and settle down somewhere.

But stained with the blood of Ned and Bill Kailer, he could never hope to do so, for old Benjamin Kailer was not the kind to give up his vengeance, not as long as he had one son left to press the search and could hire men like Amos Bell to assist him.

Of course, John Temple could put a stop to the relentless chase if he so wished. He had only to halt, face Ford Kailer and the Pinkerton man, and shoot it out with them, confident that his superior ability and the experience gained in the past years would prevail.

But that would mean two more killings—and there had already been too much blood shed. Too, he had nothing against Ford; it had been the eldest Kailer brothers who had taken part in the killing of his mother and father and the rape and murder of his young sisters. Temple figured he had settled the score for that, and he'd like for it to end there.

But vengeance only begot vengeance, he had come to realize, and the end was never truly reached until all persons involved—sometimes those only remotely touched—were dead. No, the answer was to continue with his plan of avoiding a showdown with Ford Kailer and Amos Bell, to deny himself the possibility of making Laurie his wife, and bury himself deep in Mexico.

"Going to be a mighty good feeling for me, too," he heard Morgan Cole say to his sister. "Putting you on that eastbound stage'll be a big load off my shoulders."

Laurie smiled dryly at Morgan and dabbed at the moisture on her face, which still showed traces of dust streaks.

"Don't go naming the colt before it's foaled," she said with a show of her earlier spirit. "I'm not aboard yet."

"You will be, come time," Morgan stated in a flat, positive way. "Just like Pa wants."

Laurie swept her brother with a withering look of distaste. "I've often wondered what you'll do after Pa's dead. Who is going to tell you when to blow your nose or—"

"Be enough of that!" Morgan cut in hotly, altering his position and moving threateningly toward her. "I expect I—" he continued but then broke off.

Immediately ahead three men had ridden out of the peninsula of trees that extended into the flat and halted before them. All were hard-looking, grim-faced, bearded men in worn range clothing; and each was holding a cocked pistol.

"Howdy, Clint," the one in the center said.

Temple had come to a quick stop, surprise and anger rolling through him. He had suspected all along there was more to Philbin's veiled promise of help than just talk intended to irritate Marshal Ira Kelley, but he had carelessly allowed the probability to slip his mind.

"Nate! Where in the hell have you boys been?" Philbin demanded in a harsh voice. "Was looking for you yesterday!"

"Was a humdinger of a sandstorm going on, and there was a'plenty of redskins on the loose," Nate replied coolly, "or maybe you didn't notice. Anyway, we was expecting you to be riding a stagecoach, not hoofing it. . . . You gents there, shuck your guns and throw them off into that brush on your left. Real easy, now—"

Temple hesitated a moment and then, shrugging,

133

complied. Gabriel, Morgan Cole, and the lawman in that order followed his example.

"Was the lousy damned Indians," Philbin said, explaining his predicament, and then nodded to Laurie. "Get the key out of the old man's vest pocket, missy, and unlock these irons."

The girl hesitated briefly and then did as she was directed after which she stepped quickly away from the outlaw.

Philbin, chafing his wrists vigorously, considered her thoughtfully. "I reckon you know you waited too long to do what I was asking," he said, pausing in the restoration of circulation long enough to pick up Ira Kelley's discarded weapon and thrust it under his belt. "Could rightly say you've lost your big chance."

Laurie made no comment but simply waited in silence. The outlaw turned to Nate. "You bring me a horse?"

"Waiting back there in the trees—"

"Good," Philbin said and took the pistol from his belt. "Little lady there'll be going with us. I've sort of took a shine to her—even if she didn't help me get loose like I asked."

Temple threw a hurried glance at the girl. That was what had been taking place between the two! There had been a scheme of some sort cooked up by the outlaw that involved Laurie, but she had apparently backed away from it.

"I reckon that'll suit you fine, won't it?"

At the outlaw's question, the girl shook her head. "I won't go with you—"

Philbin's dark eyes narrowed. Swiping at the sweat on his face, he said, "The hell you say! Thought you was wanting to get away from that pa of yours—"

Laurie nodded. "I do—but not with you."

134

Philbin's lips shaped into a down-curving sneer. "That so? Well, now maybe I've got the say-so about that! If I—"

"Come on, Clint, let's get the hell out of here," the rider to Nate's left said impatiently. "We've been waiting around here for you more'n a week, just—"

"All right," Philbin cut in, "but first off I've got a score to settle with this tinhorn marshal. I owe him a'plenty," he added and stepped up close to Kelley.

"Leave him alone, Philbin," Tom Gabriel said, starting to move forward but then dropping back when Nate gestured threateningly with his revolver.

"You're loose now," Temple said. "No point in taking what's happened out on the marshal."

"That's where you're wrong," the outlaw shouted and, rocking forward, clubbed Ira Kelley solidly on the side of the head with the pistol. "I got plenty to pay him back for."

Kelley staggered and dropped to hands and knees. Face down he hung there briefly, shook himself, and started to rise. Immediately Clint Philbin drew back a booted foot and drove a vicious blow into the old lawman's side. Kelley flinched as breath exploded from his lungs, but no other sound escaped him.

"Seems I recollect hearing you say you was getting me to that sheriff in Grant one way or another. Sure pleasures me to tell you that you was wrong, old man!" Philbin said and leveling the pistol in his hand at the marshal's head drew back the hammer.

In that same moment of time a gun thundered, and a ball of smoke boiled up from beneath Ira Kelley. Philbin rocked back, a look of surprise on his dark features as a quickly spreading stain of red appeared on his chest.

135

Again there was a muffled blast, coming as before from the crouched shape of the lawman.

"You ain't going nowhere 'cepting to hell!" Kelley declared. "I ain't about to turn you loose on folks—"

His words were cut short by the louder report of the pistol held in Nate's hand. Drawing himself up slightly as if determined to rise Ira Kelley paused momentarily and then with a shake of his head collapsed onto the hot sand.

As the smoke began to drift away, Nate half-turned to the two men with him, said, "Keep a eye on them jaspers," and swung down off his horse. Moving first to Philbin, lying face up in the driving sunlight, he knelt beside the outlaw and felt for a pulse.

"Deader than a fence post," he said and, rising, moved to where the lifeless body of Ira Kelley lay. "Who'd ever figured that old bastard'd be packing a belly gun?" he added and, reaching down, picked up the small twin-barreled weapon.

"Old Clint sure didn't," one of the other riders said dryly.

Nate ignored the remark. "Forty-one," he murmured absently, examining the weapon. "Reckon I'll just hang onto this here—for luck."

"Come on, Nate, let's get out of here. Them shots is bringing company."

The outlaw, thrusting the derringer into a pocket, turned at once to his horse. Beyond him Temple could see a half a dozen or so riders, apparently attracted by the firing, coming up at a fast gallop from the settlement.

"Now, you jaspers just stand easy," Nate warned, settling himself in the saddle. "We don't aim to hurt nobody, but if any of you makes a grab for one of them guns before we're out of sight in the trees—a couple of you'll die quick."

The outlaws wheeled their horses about and started for the nearby brush and large growth. Temple, catching motion on Gabriel's part, shook his head warningly.

"No—it's not worth it, Tom!"

The rancher hesitated, and then moments later Clint Philbin's friends disappeared into the trees and were lost to sight.

Morgan Cole had pivoted to face his sister, his face flushed with anger. "Was what Philbin said the truth? Was you thinking about running off with him?"

"I was," Laurie admitted coolly.

"And if you could've helped him get loose from the marshal, you would've gone?"

Temple, kneeling beside the lawman searching for a pulse he knew would not be there but making certain nevertheless, paused and waited to hear the girl's response.

"No, I decided against it."

"But you had it in your head to, didn't you?" Morgan pressed angrily. "You'd have gone off with that damned outlaw—that killer—just to spite Pa and—"

"Let it go—she's answered your question," Temple snapped, cutting into the conversation and as Laurie flashed him a grateful look, rose and faced the riders now pulling to a halt before them.

"What's going on here?" one, a cowhand from appearances, asked, staring at the dead men.

"We seen some fellows on horses," another in the party said. "Where'd they go?"

"Rode off into the trees," Gabriel explained and went into detail not only about the outlaws and the shootings but also about the trials and tribulations he

137

and the others with him had experienced in the past days and nights.

When he had finished, one of the riders whistled softly and said, "I'd say you folks've sure had your share of hell! Why don't you all just climb up behind us and let us ride you back to town—we'll send a wagon for the marshal there and that owlhoot he plugged."

Temple and the others needed no second invitation and after the weapons that had been tossed into the brush had been recovered, quickly complied.

20

Doubtful Canyon could hardly be called a town, as someone had observed earlier, Temple saw while riding double with one of the local residents when they reached the thin cluster of buildings.

"When will the next eastbound coach come in?" he heard Morgan ask the man with whom he was riding.

"Gets here about dark. Lays over till morning."

Cole shrugged disappointedly and glanced at Laurie. She was looking straight ahead, and as they pulled into the yard fronting the low rambling adobe way station, and halted, she continued to keep her eyes forward.

"Obliged to you," Temple said, sliding off the hindquarters of the horse he was on and quickly moved to the north side of the station.

Cautious, he was intentionally avoiding the entrance to the building and its waiting room. Kailer and Amos Bell could be inside. The possibility was remote, considering the Apaches and the frightful sandstorm— the worst folks had seen around there in forty years according to the man who had brought him in—but now so near to reaching the Mexican border and the safety beyond, Temple was taking nothing for granted.

As he came around the corner of the structure, he saw a young cowhand standing just beyond the way station's barn. Two horses were close by—both saddled and equipped with blanket rolls, grub sacks, and gear, ready for traveling. The man was intently watching the activity in front of the coach stop, and it came immediately to Temple that he could only be Harley Edge, the man Laurie Cole intended to meet and ride away with.

A stir of resentment moved through Temple. Edge didn't look to him like the kind of man the girl deserved. He doubted if he could ever properly care and provide for her. A frown knitted Temple's sweat-beaded brow. Hell! Laurie knew that—that was why she had turned to himself—had even considered going off with Clint Philbin! She was looking, hoping to find more than Harley Edge to make a life with.

Lord how he wished he could be that man! He hadn't realized until that moment how much she had come to mean to him—he could not deny that now. And he believed she felt the same about him. At first he had thought her interest was no more than his being a means to an end—and probably such was true at the beginning. But Temple was certain now that that had changed— that her interest had grown into a stronger feeling for him, just as his had for her.

Nothing would please and thrill him more than taking Laurie Cole to be his wife. He could visualize what it would be like to have her—so young and beautiful, so bright and alive; but he was too much of a man to succumb to his own desires and in so doing condemn her to the kind of half life he was facing.

He saw her then. She had followed him around the side of the building and now stood quietly in the shadows studying him soberly. Temple let his gaze touch her and then, nodding slightly, moved for the rear door of the way station. With him out of the way Laurie would be able to see Harley Edge waiting on beyond.

Entering the dim interior of the station, Temple saw that there were but two men present—Morgan Cole and Tom Gabriel—besides the agent. As he came through the doorway, Gabriel, sitting at a table with Cole—a plate of stew and bread and a cup of coffee before each—beckoned to him.

"Can get something to eat here, Temple! Come on—let them bring you some!"

Temple needed no further encouragement and, crossing the room, sat down beside the rancher. Almost immediately a woman appeared bringing a similar meal and placed it before him.

"Where's the girl?" she asked, glancing around.

Cole whirled about and looked over his shoulder. "Thought she was coming right behind me. I'll go—"

"Laurie's right outside," Temple said. "Expect she'll be here in a bit."

Morgan frowned, gave that thought, and then settled back down. Temple began to eat, taking time to enjoy the food despite the clamorings of his stomach.

"You the fellow that rode shotgun for Abe?"

Temple raised his head and looked the man up and down. He was a small, thin individual wearing a green eyeshade, dressed in bib overalls, a plaid shirt, and thick-soled shoes. One of the hostlers, likely.

"He's the one," Gabriel said. "This here's the station agent, Temple—Dave Christman, the man you was told to see about a horse."

Temple extended his hand which Christman shook firmly. "Was sure some job you done," the agent said admiringly.

"Was all of us doing it," Temple said and resumed his meal.

"Well, the soldiers'll put a stop to them damn Apaches raising hell," Christman said. "Got a company of cavalry coming in from Fort Bayard. They'll see to them stinking renegades. Ain't much they can do about a sandstorm, however," he added with a laugh. "That one was sure a jim-dandy! . . . You be wanting a room?"

Temple shook his head. "No, aim to head out before dark. Need a horse and gear."

"You just pick one of them animals that're in the back corral. Saddle and such will be in the barn."

"How much?"

"For you, I reckon twenty-five dollars will cover the whole works."

Temple said, "I appreciate that. Soon as I'm through eating, I'll go take a look."

"Good enough," the agent replied. "I'll write you up a bill of sale soon as you've done your choosing."

Morgan Cole rose and, features anxious, turned to the door as Christman moved off to his office and living quarters maintained in the south side of the building. Tom Gabriel, finished with his dinner, leaned back in his chair.

"Still set on heading into Mexico?"

Temple nodded. "Soon as I can get myself a horse and gear and some trail grub."

The rancher scrubbed nervously at the stubble on his chin. "Sure wish I could get my mind fixed on what I ought to do," he said in a falling voice.

"You mean about marrying the lady you told me about—the one that works in the saloon?"

"Yeh, Cinnamon. Just can't decide what I ought to do—"

"All you need do is be sure she's the woman yo want for a wife. Being married—to me, anyway— something that lasts a lifetime"

"Way I feel too, but when I get to studying about it I come up with a dozen reasons why I hadn't ough¹ t marry her."

"That's where you're making a mistake," Temple said, laying down his fork. "It's what you want that counts, so forget everybody else. Fellow once told me that if you keep putting things off until tomorrow, you'll end up finally with nothing but a stack of yesterdays—and regrets. Seems to me that's what's going to happen to you."

The cattleman continued to rub at his jaw and stare at the floor. Then, "That makes plenty of sense," he said, rising, "and I'm going to decide one way or the other today—not tomorrow. . . . Will I see you before I pull out?"

"Possible," Temple said, pushing back his plate. On past Gabriel he saw Laurie Cole approaching the door followed closely by her brother and immediately wondered briefly if Morgan had prevented the girl from meeting Harley Edge, or if Laurie, of her own volition had avoided it. Coming to his feet, Temple thrust out his hand and shook that of the rancher.

"Just in case I don't, it was good knowing you, and whatever you decide—good luck "

"Same to you," Gabriel said and turned on his heel Reaching the building's front exit, he paused long enough to let Laurie and Morgan Cole enter while nodding to each and then, stepping outside, bent his steps toward the saloon—the Monticello according to the sign above the door.

Temple glanced at the Coles as he moved by them.

143

Morgan's features were stiff and angry; Laurie appeared dispirited, and there was a lost, hopeless look in her eyes as she sat down at a table in the center of the room.

"I want you to eat," Temple heard Morgan Cole say in a hard voice. "Then you're to stay right here—inside the way station. Won't be no stage going east till morning, so I'll get you a room for the night."

Laurie nodded woodenly and let her attention drift to Temple. He read the appeal in her eyes, the hope that he had changed his thinking, that they could make a life together. Unable to meet her steady gaze longer than a moment or two, Temple pivoted on his heel and left the building by the doorway he had entered.

Harley Edge had moved to the far side of the barn, he noted, as he sought out the corral mentioned by Dave Christman. Selecting a tough, well set-up buckskin gelding, Temple led the animal into the barn, picked out a saddle, blanket, bridle, and other necessary gear, and put it on the horse That done, he rode the gelding back to the rear of the way station, tied him to a post, and then went in search of Christman and the bill of sale that he would need

Morgan Cole was no longer in the dining area of the station, and Laurie still alone, was at her table, picking indifferently at the meal that had been set before her. She looked up as he entered, but Temple, refusing to punish himself any further, continued on into the adjoining area into which he had seen Christman disappear. The agent was there, sitting at a large rolltop desk. He had the paper covering the sale of the horse all ready except for entering the description and the brand.

The bill completed, Temple handed over the money necessary to close the sale, retraced his steps into the

144

combination waiting and dining room, and turned hurriedly for the rear door. Only then did he notice that Laurie Cole was no longer at her table, nor was she to be seen anywhere. He swore raggedly.

This time Laurie would go to Harley Edge. Morgan was absent, busy elsewhere. Getting no response from himself, Temple realized, the girl had made her decision; she was going through with her intentions to leave with the cowhand.

It was too bad. While he believed in a man or a woman choosing their own way of life, he felt that Laurie would have done better doing as her pa had asked and not settling for Harley Edge. But she had not seen it that way. Shrugging, Temple moved on for the door and the horse he had waiting in the yard. He'd not soon forget Laurie Cole; she would be in his mind for the rest of his life he reckoned, and there'd always be that haunting regret that he could not have made her his own.

Pushing the screen door open, Temple stepped out into the driving sunlight—and came to an abrupt halt Standing beside the buckskin was Laurie, and talking to Harley Edge over near the barn were two men. It took but a quick glance to recognize both; one was Ford Kailer, the other Amos Bell.

21

John Temple stiffened, and a bleakness filled his eyes. Slowly his shoulders came down as if surrendering, finally, to frustration and the inevitable. . . . All those long, lonely days and nights in country where it was never prudent to make a friend; all those weary, endless miles on the trail, some replete with danger, some with nothing more than monotony—only to have it all go for nothing on the very day when he was within hours of Mexico and the sanctuary it offered.

"Are those the two men you have been running from?"

Laurie's tense voice brought his attention to her. The question irritated him. He was not running from Bell and Kailer in the sense that he feared them. It was only that he wanted no showdown and resultant killing. But he let it pass

"That's them," he said. "Must've just ridden in—or maybe they've been here. Could've been in the saloon or somewhere when we were brought in."

"I'm sorry," Laurie said gently. "I know how much you wanted to get to Mexico. It was the accident and the windstorm that let them catch up with you."

He nodded "I reckon that was it."

She looked again at the two men still in conversation

with Edge. "Is there anything I can do to help you, Temple? Maybe I could talk to them and delay them somehow."

He smiled down at her, thinking how lovely she looked in that moment despite all she had been through—and how much he would miss her when she was no longer around.

"Obliged for the offer, but there's not much you could do. My only chance is to mount up and ride out—and gamble on them not spotting me when I do."

"Maybe," she said quickly, "if I were with you—a man and a woman leaving—they wouldn't think anything of it."

Temple frowned as he gave that thought. Immediately Laurie took heart. "I want so bad to go with you! It isn't that you're just a way out for me. It's that I love you, Temple—I truly do—and if I lose you there'll be nothing ahead for me—not ever."

"Can't say that I feel any different about you, but the kind of life I've got to offer—" He broke off, a wry grin parting his lips. "Fact is, with them showing up, I don't have anything to offer."

Laurie brushed at her eyes. "Can't you talk to them? Make them see that—"

"Talking was done a long time ago. Old Ben Kailer, the father of the two I shot and of Ford, won't quit until he sees me swinging from a gallows."

"But it's all so wrong!" she protested. "You shouldn't have to keep running on and on, hiding from them, like you have been. You killed those Kailers because they killed your sisters—your whole family. I don't hold with taking someone else's life, but I think you were justified. Why can't you just call a halt here and now to this—this ridiculous chase, talk to those two men and make them understand that—''

Temple silenced the girl with a shake of his head. "They'd not listen—and it would end up with more killing, and I've done enough of that for one lifetime.''

Laurie bit at her lower lip. "But wouldn't it be worth a try? I could go to them, tell them you want to talk things over and see if you can't settle things without bloodshed. They just might listen.''

"Already said I doubt if they'd listen. They haven't tracked me all over the country just to sit down and jaw about what's happened.''

"You don't know that. Maybe they're as sick of all that hunting for you as you are sick of running from them, and you could strike a bargain with them—promise them you'd go down into Mexico, and they'd never see you again.''

Temple gave that thought. He doubted Laurie or anyone else could reason with Ford Kailer, but he reckoned it was worth a try. Chances were there'd be a showdown before he could get clear of the town, anyway, so there would be nothing lost.

"Please, Temple—for my sake—''

"I'm willing," he said. "Tell them I'll meet them at that corral back of the barn.''

Eyes bright with tears, Laurie nodded. "I'll go right away," she said and then paused. "If—if you could only get things straightened out with them so there'd be no need to go to Mexico.''

"No—''

"And there can be something for us—a life—''

His lean face was sober as he looked closely at her. "Best you be sure that's what you want. I won't have you settling for me as a way out—as the answer to

148

getting loose from your pa. You've got to be certain that—"

"I'm certain," Laurie broke in and, moving up to him quickly, kissed him on the lips. Turning away, she started for the far corner of the barn where Kailer and Bell stood talking with Harley Edge.

"Laurie—come back here!"

At Morgan Cole's shouted command the girl paused and then, shaking her head, hurried on.

"Damn it—I'll show her who—"

"You won't show her nothing," Temple cut in.

"Well, by God, I'm not letting her go off with that no-account drifter—"

"She's not."

Cole stared at Temple. "Then what the hell's she doing?"

"If you want to know, come along with me," Temple said and crossed to the horse corral.

Shortly, with Laurie leading the way, Kailer and the Pinkerton detective—trailed by Harley Edge—rounded the far corner of the barn and moved toward Temple and Cole, waiting at the corral.

Kailer, tall, thin-faced, head thrust forward, sharp eyes intent, slowed perceptibly when he saw Morgan Cole with Temple, but Laurie, half-turning, reassured him, apparently stating that the second man was her brother and was in no way involved in the matter. At that Ford Kailer had resumed stride.

Reaching the corral, Kailer again slowed and allowed Bell to move up beside him while Laurie hurried to stand next to Temple, who immediately shook his head.

"Best you not be close. I won't have you hurt if this comes down to gunplay."

Kailer took that up at once. "Just what it's going to do unless you're willing to come back with me—"

"Not a chance," Temple said evenly, hands dropping to his sides as he settled forward. "I want to talk and see if we can patch this thing up without any more killing. Otherwise—"

"Time for talking's long gone—"

'Maybe, and maybe it shouldn't be," Temple said. 'I'm sorry for your sake and your pa's sake that your brothers are dead—but I'm not sorry I killed them. They had it coming."

"That's how you see it!" Kailer snapped. "There was a lot of that that happened after that fool Ewing put out an order for those folks to move. Why didn't you go out and shoot all the other guerrillas and army deserters who done burning and murdering?"

"It was your brothers and two of their friends that killed my family. My quarrel was with them."

"It's with me now. You're a convicted killer, sentenced by a judge to hang—but one of them friends of yours fixed it so's you could escape. I'm taking you back and seeing to it personally that you swing."

"Not likely," Temple said dryly. "I was hoping you'd be a reasonable man, but I can see you're not. . . . Now, I don't want to shoot you, Kailer. Been dodging doing it for a long time, although it would've been easy. You forget about that gun you're wearing— goes for you, too, detective. I'm climbing on my horse and riding out. If either one of you tries to stop me, I'll kill you."

Ford Kailer made no reply but simply stared at Temple, his eyes burning with hate. Amos Bell nodded, signifying his understanding. Then, glancing at Laurie, his features strained and heavy with regret, John Temple pivoted slowly and began to retrace his steps to his waiting horse.

"Temple!" Laurie screamed.

As her cry of alarm split the hot silence of the afternoon, Temple spun. The pistol nestled in the holster on his hip seemed to leap magically into his hand. It bucked sharply as it blasted its bullet, the sound overriding that of the weapon held by Ford Kailer which came out a split second later.

Kailer stiffened, a pained look on his face, eyes spreading with surprise. Abruptly the pistol in his hand dropped, and, twisting about slowly, he fell to the ground.

A savage anger was rushing through Temple. He had hoped to avoid gunplay and had failed. But a determination was also flowing through him now—a decision to put the Kailer matter behind him once and for all time. Crouched, smoke trickling from the barrel of his weapon, he fixed his eyes on the Pinkerton man, standing with hands raised above his head.

"You aim to take it up from here?"

Bell shook his head. "It's ended far as I'm concerned

"Little hard to believe that," Temple said. "His pa hired you to find me. He won't let it end."

"Ben Kailer ain't got no say where he is," Bell replied, lowering his hands cautiously. "Died almost a year ago. This thing should've ended right then, but Ford wouldn't let it. Had his mind set on tracking you down and killing you—if it took the rest of his life."

"Killing me?"

"What he figured to do '

Temple straightened slowly, pistol still in his hand With old Ben Kailer dead, matters would change—but the law would not forget. He was an escaped criminal, one that had been sentenced to hang.

"Where does this leave you?"

Amos Bell shrugged. "I'm out of it. Was hired by the Kailers to find you. Done my job—and now they're both gone, so that's it."

'You're not interested in taking me back so's the law can finish what it started? Probably a reward—"

"I've got nothing to do with you being an escaped criminal. Up to the law to skin their own cats. Anyway, I don't think you need worry about that. Ben Kailer told the court to leave you to him—that he'd see to it you were caught and brought back—so they did nothing about it. Expect the law won't even remember you."

Several men, attracted by the gunshots, had hurried up from the way station and were standing around talking in low voices and wondering what had taken place. Harley Edge and Bell became the center of their curiosity.

Temple, tension gone, relief running through him, nolstered his pistol and turned to Laurie. At once she came hurrying to him. He reached out, took the girl's shoulders in his hands, and looked closely at her.

'Guess we know where I stand now. What about you—are you still sure?"

She nodded. "I am—and I'm ready to go anywhere with you—Mexico, if you say."

Temple smiled 'Can make a choice now," he said and came about to face Morgan Cole but paused.

Approaching at a fast walk, an attractive red-haired woman clinging to his arm, was Tom Gabriel. Apparently also curious about the shooting, they were coming to see what it was all about. Both were smiling happily, and when the rancher caught Temple's eye, he nodded vigorously. Evidently Tom Gabriel had made his decision

"Cole," Temple said, swinging back to Morgan "I'll make this short and sweet. I'm taking Laurie with me. We'll be married soon as we can find a preacher—probably in Franklin."

Morgan Cole's face flushed with anger. "You're doing what? Pa wants her to—"

"I'm not interested in what he wants, and I don't want any trouble with you, so don't start any. Laurie's going with me—even if I have to fight you for her."

Morgan swiped at the sweat on his forehead with the back of his hand and glanced about at the crowd, all looking on with interest. He shrugged.

"All right—take her, and damned good riddance far as I'm concerned! She ain't been nothing but trouble for me ever since she grew up, and it'll be a mighty big relief not to have to watch over her any more."

"Can tell your pa that it'll be me watching out for her from now on and that I'll take good care of her. She'll never want for anything long as there's breath in my body."

Cole again brushed at his face. "She's your problem, mister. I'm done with it—done with her and with kissing Pa's backside. I figure if she's got the guts to go through with what she started to do—I can do some changing too."

Laurie crossed quickly to her brother, threw her arms about his neck, and hugged him. "I'm glad to hear that, Morg—glad you're finally going to have an understanding with Pa. I can't remember you ever doing anything you wanted. It was always what he wanted."

"Won't be that way from now on. . . . When will you be riding out?"

"Soon as I can get a horse and gear for Laurie," Temple replied.

She smiled at him. "There's no big hurry, Temple. You're through with running—but I can't go on calling you Temple! What's your given name?"

"John—and you're right " he said, putting his arm around her. "From here on we'll start living the way folks are supposed to—staying out of trouble, and doing a lot of loving "